About the Author

Behrouz was born in 1980 in Leeds, England, was raised by two Iranian parents and grew up primarily in Ottawa, Canada; a self-professed 'cultural mutt.' He was a teacher of English as a second language for four years and has worked as an accountant for a dental support organisation for the last seven years, but his first love has always been art, primarily cinema and literature. After self-publishing his first novella, *Iranian Tango, Canadian Waltz*, as an experiment in 2015, he has now written his first 'proper' novella. He currently resides in Ottawa with his wife and daughter.

A Brown Person's Guide to Living in Canada

Behrouz Mostaghaci

A Brown Person's Guide to Living in Canada

Olympia Publishers
London

www.olympiapublishers.com
OLYMPIA PAPERBACK EDITION

Copyright © Behrouz Mostaghaci 2023

The right of Behrouz Mostaghaci to be identified as author of this work has been asserted in accordance with sections 77 and 78 of the Copyright, Designs and Patents Act 1988.

All Rights Reserved

No reproduction, copy or transmission of this publication may be made without written permission. No paragraph of this publication may be reproduced, copied or transmitted save with the written permission of the publisher, or in accordance with the provisions of the Copyright Act 1956 (as amended).

Any person who commits any unauthorised act in relation to this publication may be liable to criminal prosecution and civil claims for damage.

A CIP catalogue record for this title is available from the British Library.

ISBN: 978-1-80439-170-9

This is a work of fiction.
Names, characters and incidents originate from the writer's imagination. Any resemblance to actual persons, living or dead, is purely coincidental.

First Published in 2023

Olympia Publishers
Tallis House
2 Tallis Street
London
EC4Y 0AB

Printed in Great Britain

Dedication

To my wife, Casey, and daughter, Melody, for honouring me with their incandescent love every day. To my father, Hamid, and mother, Masoumeh, for their unconditional and relentless belief in me. She can see me from up above; of that I am certain. And to all the libraries of my youth where I encountered smelly, yellow pages of great literature that quietly taught me things I didn't understand yet.

CHAPTER ONE

'Do you want to let her sleep?'

'I'm not sure…'

'It's probably okay… do you think she'll be able to sleep through the night if she sleeps now?'

'I think so.'

'She doesn't typically nap in the middle of the day any more though. She dropped her two naps, went to one nap and she's all about no naps now. Do you think it's wise?'

'I'm thinking yes. She's exhausted. She needs it.'

'Do you think we wake her up and we sing Disney songs? We'll do "I Just Can't Wait To Be King" and then do the weird Elton John version she laughs at.'

'No, we're not waking her up.'

'She only just dropped. Maybe she just needs to wipe the dust off… I don't wanna fuck up her sleep pattern.'

'She's five. I think she'll be okay.'

'You're not the one who puts her to sleep. When she gets these naps, she takes forever to go down.'

'I'll put her down then tonight.'

'You always say that and then it's the same shit. Can you put her down? I'm exhausted… no shit, so am I but I hit the nuclear auxiliary button and wind it up and get it done no matter how much running around she does.'

'You're Mr Perfect I know.'

'I'm not Mr Perfect. But we gotta be on point. You either do it or you don't.'

'Just let her nap.'

'For like how long?'

'An hour. Hour and a half?'

'What?'

'Fuuuuuuuck, Darius… you're being a helicopter parent.'

'I hate that fucking term, you know that. It's just a trash name shitty parents came up with to denigrate parents who actually give a shit about their kids. But, their kids are "tough", right? Gotta be tough. We want our kids to be tough so they can get out in the world and be independent. We don't want them to be pussy Millennials, right? God, what a trash narrative that is…'

'Okay, so we're letting her nap.'

'Fucking whatever. I think it's a mistake. Her sleep pattern is perfect and I think a long nap is a mistake. Daylight savings already shit on her pattern for a week. By the way, when are they getting rid of that shit? Is it about farmers or some shit? I'm so sick of that… and nobody says anything about it. They just adjust their clocks like automatons twice a year for no good fucking reason.'

'Are you good to drive, right now? You sound tired.'

'Macy, I'm good.'

'She'll be okay, Darius. Let her sleep. The girl needs it. Let her drift for a bit… we haven't had her nap back there like the old days when we went for midnight drives.'

'It feels like a lifetime ago. Hot damn, man… those days were fucking crazy. How did we get through it? I feel like I've repressed some of those late nights. I feel like I only remember patches.'

'God, I know… she wouldn't latch onto my nipples cuz she was tongue-tied.'

'Oh yeah, the nurses and doctors didn't think that bit of info was worth mentioning to us. Daisy missed out on the colostrum. The good stuff. Bunch of assholes.'

'And she couldn't sleep much cuz of the reflux.'

'Shit, that's right. So the doctors didn't let us know about the tongue-tie or the fact that she was having problems eating cuz of reflux. Nice. Those tax dollars of ours going to some serious education. I'm convinced that nobody who works in a professional environment gives a shit about their job, and doesn't care if anyone knows it either. People are so brazen about how inept they are, it's like what the fuck? God, I sound like my brother, right now. Jesus, I gotta check myself a bit.'

'That did sound like him!'

'Well, at least the doctors gave us gripe water. You know, serious solutions to serious problems. Hard-won strategies learnt in paediatric school or wherever the fuck they bought their diplomas.'

'Just drive, you fucking retard.'

'Yes, ma'am. That I can do… you good back there, my love? Sleep, beautiful.'

Just breathe. You need to keep your shit together, remember that. Breathe it out, bro, breathe it out. Don't let the pandemic wreck you. Macy's good. Daisy's good. I'm good. You gotta be on point. You can't lose your shit. If you do, they will.

We love being with each other so we're good. It would be nice to get some help though. We don't have anybody to help us. It's just the three of us. But, other parents get some help sometimes. Maybe the grandparents, aunts or uncles could watch the child for one day. Just one day. We've had Daisy home since the first pandemic lockdown. It's been fifteen months. Fifteen months since Macy and I had a day to ourselves. That is so fucked up. But, others have gone through worse. Yeah, but that doesn't mean I'm not tired.

I've loved the time home with my family. It's been beautiful. Gorgeous. Daisy has improved so much since being home. Her reading, her writing, all the one-on-one learning. It's been astounding. We're tired though. Macy and I are on from seven a.m. to nine p.m. I mean like fucking on. We can't rest until Daisy goes to bed. There's no physical break. No mental break. We're on right from the jump. It's built character. I'm tired though. Honestly, the home time has been amazing. No commute. Incredible environmental gains. Financial gains from not driving. No rushing in the morning to get to work.

But Daisy misses her friends. And Macy and I are tired. We have no help. We need a break. It really has been wonderful when I look at it from a macro point of view. We're homebodies so there's nobody we love being around more than our tight family unit – just the three of us. It's all true. No lies. Macy and Daisy are the loves of my life. The lockdowns didn't bother us much since we love being home together anyway. We're still tired though. Maybe the pandemic will end soon. I'm tired. It's a red light. Stop the car. My body is tired.

'Macy, wake me up when the light turns green.'

CHAPTER TWO

Daisy wasn't the only one who nodded off. Macy's head was doing that awkward half-asleep up-down drift where the chin won't allow itself to touch the person's chest so keeps icing upwards with a jolt. God, what is that about anyway? Why do people do things like that? Aren't there better ways to get a nap? Maybe adjust the seat back so you've got some lean? And then your head can plant itself on the headrest, leave a permanent grease spot on the black leather, and then allow your mouth to slowly morph into a dead fish pose; always an attractive look.

That's Pinecrest Cemetery. While my girls were momentarily visiting the other side, I took a look at my mom's resting place. Should I turn in there and check it out? It's been a while since I've visited. If you visit a lot, does that mean the person meant more to you? If you don't visit, does that make you a soulless android? If you just visit on Mother's Day, does that make you a contrived stooge? I dunno. I wouldn't say I visit a lot but it's been ten years, shit almost eleven years, since she left. I've probably been here a dozen times.

If I turn in there and park, the girls might wake up. Macy wants Daisy to nap a bit. If I disturb that notion, she'll get pissed with me. What if I turn into the cemetery but keep the car moving? Yeah, I'll do that. They'll never know we stopped in here.

I pulled in and saw the usual cemetery foliage. Would it kill cemetery owners to switch it up a bit? Perhaps a pop art cemetery? Maybe keep the foliage but paint it all black? This place is big though. Macy's grandparents are resting in a cemetery on Prince of Wales; I forget the name. It's on the way to North Gower, I think. They're not stones; they're the kind where it's like a steel plate in the ground with a hole that you can plant flowers and water into.

Pinecrest Cemetery is pretty hardcore though. Lots of rolling hills like we've stepped into Ireland; or what I imagine Ireland to be. Never actually been there but maybe, someday, I can go there with the girls and we can bask in the glory of all that green. It would be glorious. And have real Guinness from some charming old taverns with people breaking out into song. I'm not sure it'd really be like that though. Maybe the Guinness would be swill and people were so beaten down by socio-economic stress that they'd rather punch me in the mouth than sing a showstopper.

Such a handsome cemetery though. I slowly roamed through the little winding roads and clocked my surroundings. Not many people here though. I wonder what people do here anyway. They come for the peace, perhaps? They come to remember? Out of obligation? Guilt? To reconnect with the pain?

I remember when it all happened. My mom was diagnosed with ovarian cancer in November 2008 with a walnut-sized death sentence handed to her by a German oncologist. After a slew of false hope declarations sadly sprinkled on the forest ground like breadcrumbs, she was eventually led to the witch's gingerbread house, fattened up (or in reality, starved out) and tossed into the wood burning oven to join the cavalcade of the dearly forgotten in this cemetery here.

Her stone is pretty nice though. I feel bad for families that want a stone but can't afford one. It's sad that even death becomes a lucrative racket. Not a very original thought but worth mentioning anyway. Even in death, we're fighting for status.

It says 'Together Forever' on the stone. Not my choice. I probably would have chosen something less canned. Mom probably would've laughed at that hammy sentiment. There aren't just stones here; there are full-on mausoleums. Daaaamn.

I was walking through here with the girls a year ago and it's interesting to see the death dates on the stones. Some die within a year of each other like they were true soul mates. Some single stones have an eerily short duration between birth and death which makes us think it's either a) car crash, b) cancer, or c) suicide. What else could it be? Some sort of rare condition, perhaps?

I continued driving around. The girls still out; Daisy, completely out, poor beautiful thing. And Macy still working on the neck yo-yo sleep strategy. Quite comical actually. How many times can her head go up and down like that? It's bananas.

I still think about Mom every day. That's weird, isn't it? Like every day. It's conditioned at this point, I think. Sometimes, she'll pop into my head at a completely arbitrary moment and I'll slip into a ten-second reverie, after getting back to whatever I was doing. She'll whisper in my ear. There was a line in an old movie, the title I can't remember, where the guy says he likes the pain after a break-up. The pain keeps him close to the one he's lost. Those pangs keep that person not just alive in memory but close by. Without the hurt, the person slowly starts to evaporate into the ether. People like saying 'ether', don't they? It seems like the most interesting thing to float up into if I knew what the hell 'ether' was. I could look it up. I won't say the 'G' word for looking something up because the fact that it's a verb now makes my skin crawl.

At my mom's funeral, it was one of those clear blue days that make you feel like you're inside a baby blue dome you could play baseball in. Not a whiff of cloud cover anywhere. The funeral director, or whoever he was, recited something from some book that may have been Corinthians (not sure what that is) and then I delivered a short eulogy. I hoped it was interesting and I promised myself I wouldn't cry, which I didn't. No prayers; Mom didn't want any. She was a spiritual creature but not one for the organised stuff, bless her.

For a few years, I'd stop by Pinecrest to see her. I could hear the cars whizzing down Baseline on their way to Ikea. How can that place be full every day of the year? Are there that many people that need furniture and home décor upgrades that often? How can it be teeming with vain rats on the daily? And yet it is.

Every time I visited Mom, I'd bring my book of Rimbaud poems with me. How pretentious is that! I didn't mean for it to be but it gave me a feeling of serenity. I'd sit next to her resting place and I'd read poems from the master. Bastard wasn't even twenty when he wrote those things. My goodness. I'd open the book and read random passages out loud, cross-legged, and I'd feel ants crawling on me and mosquitos trying to nick me. Never a fan of creepy crawlies, at her side, it's the only time I just let them crawl all over me. I just was too peaceful to care. I'd read those metaphysical and sometimes perverse lines from that impudent Charleville punk and I'd feel okay afterwards. Looking back on that, I can't believe I did that. It seems so studied but I really did do it and left feeling okay. Tears would stain the pages. I wonder if the pages have that wet-wrinkled afterglow if I looked now?

Bad things happening to wonderful people makes me feel like goo. Mom was an angel. She could be hyper-critical, vain and completely irrational, but in things that actually mattered, she really was the best. I was too much of a moron in those days to realise how hard it must've been for her being in a house with three males. Why couldn't it have been one of the three of us to go? She should've been chosen to stay. The Grand Designer really whiffed there.

I continued driving. Amazing what motion does for a child in the throes of sleep. The second you stop, they feel it and their eyes magically uncork. On my way out, I knew Mom's grave was above the first hill so I wouldn't be able to see it, but it was surely there; not going anywhere. My mom was different from my dad. He speaks in a combination of Farsi and English to me and I always answer in English. But, my mom would always speak in Farsi. It was comforting. I wish Dad would do that.

'What does it feel like over there?'

'Over where?' (translated from Farsi)

'In the void.'

'Ah, the void. It doesn't feel like anything. I don't even know I'm in it. The blackness you feel from the second you sleep to the moment you wake up; that's what I feel now. That's what I think now. Blackness. I am blackness for eternity.'

'Fuck. That is the scariest thing I've ever heard.'

'It would be scary if I knew I was here.'

'What do you last remember?'

'Hospital bed. Vomiting. Sterilised linen smell. Vomit smell. Your voices in the far-off distance.'

'You could hear us?'

'I could hear something. Or it could've been the Dilaudid. It's all that helped me not think about the end.'

'But the second you started taking it, you were gone already.'

'I needed to feel good. Feel calm. You can't imagine what it feels like to be in a room with your husband and two sons, and know you won't ever see them again.'

Silence.

'How are you?'

'I'm good. Would you believe me if I told you a deadly disease ripped the world apart and everybody needed to get vaccinated and we'll probably wear masks for the rest of our lives?'

'What?'

'I'm just kidding. Stupid joke… I just wish you could've seen me become a man.'

'Yes, you were very immature.'

'Haha. It's true. I feel like you left before you actually got to see me grow up. Become a professional. Become a husband. Become a father. You would've loved Macy and Daisy. You're a lot like them. I feel you inside them.'

'What is all this bullshit you're talking about?'

'I'm telling you the truth.'

'Sounds like a lot of romantic-sounding bullshit to me.'

'Sometimes, I imagine that you never died but were just in a coma. And after eleven years, you somehow miraculously came out of it, and you walked into our house and you saw Daisy, almost six years old, sitting at the dining table eating lunch, with her unicorn T-shirt and high ponytail. And I'd say, with a tear in my eye, "This is your granddaughter." And you wouldn't be able to contain yourself and you'd explode in tears of joy. I have that fantasy all the time.'

'Oh my God, shut the fuck up!'

As I exited the gates of Pinecrest Cemetery, I turned right, as I hated doing the dart across to the left-hand lane with all those lunatic drivers zig-zagging back and forth, and heard Macy waking up as we hit one of Ottawa's eighty million potholes.

'How long was I out?'

'Not long. Daisy's still out. I guess we'll let her drift.'

'Did we just come out of Pinecrest? Where are we? Baseline?'

'Yeah. Just said hi to Mom.'

'How was she?'

'Belligerent... but good.'

Macy's eyes beamed starlight. She placed her hand on my right hand, as it dangled lazily from the five o'clock position of the New England Patriots-covered steering wheel.

CHAPTER THREE

It was on the Mackenzie King Bridge that the three of us encountered a guy who appeared to be fucked up on something… somewhere in that space he was in at the time. We marched across the bridge on our way out of Rideau Centre, the snow crunching beneath our tired feet and lower backs, almost deafening. When the air is still, that mid-February boom every step you take is jarring.

We're waiting for the 95 to take us to the Park 'n' Ride where we parked the Rogue. Macy spots a guy across the bridge, panhandling, and then going back and forth with passersby, and then spinning around in ever-decreasing circles.

'I think he's on something.' That's Macy's favourite line whenever someone seems out of sorts. An old buddy of mine from Syria would charmingly describe it this way: 'I think he must be on high.'

I didn't get impressed, anxious or interested in these sights any more. Not because I was incredibly seasoned, but only because I had seen so much of this craziness. When I stayed in New York for a few months when I was twenty-four, I was regularly accosted by bizarros whose MO I could never quite figure out. My roommate at the time, who was usually with me, would utter in his inimitable Pennsylvanian twang, 'That was overwhelming.' It indeed was at first. When a silver-haired geriatric grabs your arm and yells, 'Don't look at my girlfriend!' you can't help but feel a bit shaky. Especially when there is no girlfriend in sight.

After that stint in NYC hardened me a bit, my few years spent living in the St. Laurent Boulevard apartments, right across from a Loblaws parking lot that featured a horrific 'honour killing' within viewing distance from where I resided on the seventeenth, allowed me to complete my maturation from the babe in the woods I once was. There were Ottawa Housing projects all around me. That's the weird thing about Ottawa; there isn't one bad neighbourhood that you can point to and say stay away from that hole. The city is replete with rough areas but they're all democratically distributed. It allows for all socio-economic classes to touch the scrub and shine of quotidian Ottawa life.

'He's crossing the bridge.' Macy was worried and put her hand on Daisy's chest, tugging her a little closer in.

'Macy, chill. These guys are harmless. You put a finger on them and they fall over.'

'You don't know if he has a knife or what.'

'Yeah, I'll watch for that.'

'Darius, he's coming right at us.'

'You don't need to have Daisy so close to you right now. Take your hand off her front and just keep it behind her hip.'

The guy was definitely not all there but who's to say where he was, how he got there and where he was going. Maybe he was on some shit, perhaps just a delusional hobo, or just a lazy asshole putting on an act for all the tourists who'd love to take a selfie with an authentic vagrant in the nation's capital; these guys were practically performance artists.

He walked up, or clumsily staggered would be more appropriate, to our trio. I could smell booze on him, which is par for the course when you encounter these bozos, and he also had a mixed aroma of cigarettes (he might've just smoked one), shit (he might've just taken one) and something I couldn't put my finger on. Maybe earwax.

The guy suddenly transformed from fatigued wanderer to adrenalized keynote speaker. 'I should knock that toque right off your head!'

I was wearing a hat brandishing the logo of the New England Patriots, a team that is very much a love/hate proposition for most NFL fans, and even casuals who don't know shit about football.

'Yeah, I get that. I'm a fan. I've been a fan for over twenty years now. Sorry, dude.'

I looked him right in the eye and never looked down. But, not always right into his pupils. More kind of a combination of sharp eye contact, so he knew I wasn't afraid or intimidated by him, and an unfocused looking past him style, to show him I wasn't staring him down and judging him.

'The league wants those assholes to win every year!'

'Yeah, you're probably right. We got lucky last week.'

'Fuck off!'

Macy braced herself quietly, but I just laughed. The guy was picking up on the fact that I was trying to placate him so he'd bugger off. Admitting that my own team got lucky in the Superbowl, when it was anything but, was something he caught. Then he surprised me.

'Hey, sorry for swearing in front of your little one.'

Maybe he did pick up on me trying to relate to him and knock my own team in the spirit of false modesty, but he did realise he had loudly sworn in front of Daisy. He was in our realm enough to know that that was not acceptable behaviour. But the problem was that he was aware that Daisy was there which gave me a tinge of worry. This guy looked and sounded erratic.

'Hey, it's okay, we've said worse.'

Not true at all. We never swore in front of Daisy. Parents who do, I think, are disrespectful assholes. Not that I would call my parents that exactly but they did allow my brother and I to swear non-stop in the house and, looking back on it, it was abhorrent. Nobody's saying to run your household like a Midnight Mass séance, but letting expletives fly in the house is a sign of a serious collapse.

'Dude, you don't look totally well. You good? I saw you across the bridge kinda spinning.'

'Yeah, I'm okay but I haven't eaten in a couple of days and I had a seizure. You got any change?'

While I was talking to this guy, he had about thirty per cent of my attention. The remainder was devoted to knowing exactly where Macy and Daisy were in relation to this guy. Just on the off-chance, the one per cent chance, this guy flipped out a knife, I needed to know how quickly I could disable him and what his proximity to my girls was. They were fine and I wasn't worried but I was getting a headache navigating this space. The atmosphere was bitterly cold but also airless; like standing on top of Mont Tremblant, with nothing but the sound of your own breathing filling the void. I say that not really knowing what Mont Tremblant feels like. I've never skied or snowboarded in my life. Few Brown people do. I think. And the ones that do are probably actually white. Like my brother. But, he can't ski either. Even if he gives the impression that he does.

'Sorry bro, we don't have any change. Just plastic. Tell you what. How 'bout we take you inside and get you a muffin or coffee or hot chocolate from Timmy's.'

'No, I don't know.'

'Come on, let us hook you up.'

'I'm gonna catch this bus.'

The 95 rolled up and he climbed on. The driver looked at us and I gestured that we'd grab the next one. It was like we were at a restaurant and I gestured to the waiter, 'Cheque, please.' Except I had never seen anyone do that before.

Daisy, in her perfectly wide-eyed manner, said, 'Daddy, why was that man being so silly?'

'He wasn't feeling well, love. And lots of other reasons but we can talk about that when you're grown up. How 'bout we go inside and wait for the next bus? And maybe get some popcorn?'

Daisy lit up and started hopping on the spot. Macy smiled. Amazing how the presence of unpredictable dread can be quashed by a bucket of yellow popcorn. That's power.

CHAPTER FOUR

Daisy was still floating on a satin pillow, her head all the way back in her car seat, legs dangling and her mouth slightly open, slightly curious.

'My God, she's so beautiful.'

'I know,' I smiled.

'Should we be saying that? Like should we say that in front of her?'

'Probably not. We can from time to time in a loving way but best to not say it too much so she doesn't get narcissistic.'

'She's always asking me to do Snapchat with her and when we look at all the pics, she only wants to see the ones of her.'

I laughed. 'That's okay. It's normal. What kid doesn't love seeing an image of themselves. Especially all those weird filters.'

'I was on IG and there are these girls I used to dance with and I think they're like grooming their kids to do modelling.'

'That's so fucked up.'

'I know right!'

'Cuz that's really what you want for your kids. To exploit them for money and to make them think that their looks are the most important thing.'

'It's so disgusting.'

'And people are always like, well it's a really good opportunity. For what? Opportunity for what? To make money off your kid? To allow them to enter a world full of materialistic assholes. Yeah, fantastic opportunity. Parents winning.'

'Why do most people even become parents?'

'I really don't know, Mace. The more I grow up, the more I respect the polarities. People who really, really want to be parents like us. And people who really, really don't want to be parents. I respect people who know what they want and really have a passion to do it.'

'Are Millennials better parents?'

'I think they probably are but there are dogshit ones in that pack as well.'

'But at least they're like more into sensitive issues and taking their time instead of being bullies.'

'Totally. I think that's true.'

'Like Baby Boomer parents were like non-existent. They're old school and into being tough and kicking the kids out at seventeen.'

'Yeah.'

'And Gen-Xers are kind of shit too.'

'They really are. It's weird. You would think Gen-Xers would've taken that rebelliousness they had towards their Baby Boomer parents and channelled it into good parenting but they're just as shitty as their folks. They just don't wanna be parents.'

'I feel like parents are too into stuff like gender reveal parties and having these massive themed birthday parties.'

'God, I know. Those wack-ass gender reveal parties. What the fuck are those all about? And push presents. What is all this shit?'

'Oh my God, all of my old dance friends do that stuff.'

'Today's parents think they're doing an amazing job if they put their kids in swimming at an early age because it "gives confidence and can save your life." Yeah, a lot of things can give you confidence besides swimming and save your life? What is that shit? What are we living on houseboats in the Great Barrier Reef? What predicament will you find yourself in where you're drifting in the middle of the ocean or stuck in a riptide? And swimming, in both of those instances, will not save your life. It will only prolong the agony before death.'

Macy was laughing to herself, charmingly, with her soft pink-tinged nails covering her mouth. She loved when I went on these rants. It wasn't an angry rant. Just a comically exasperated one. I knew it was okay when she was laughing. But, if she wasn't, I knew I was sounding like a misanthropic blowhard. In the clear for now.

'So swimming is all-important to these Karens. What else? Oh yeah, they want their kids to be "tough". No matter what, there is no situation in which they want their kids feeling any fear or anxiety of any kind. Fall and smack your face on the pavement, no problem, get up and be tough. Crying because you're two years old and you don't feel comfortable sitting in a dental chair for the first time. Too bad, suck it up and be tough. You feel a bit shy on your first day of school, too bad, get out there and meet everybody and don't show any fear or weakness. It's like these parents want their kids to become ninja masters.'

Macy was laughing even harder now. I didn't think it was that funny but if she was laughing, I was happy.

'And parents for sure want to be on top of things when it comes to their kids' internal body temperatures. If it's too hot out, hey you need to put on your hat and Crocs. It's too cold out, make sure you put on your toque and mitts. And splash pants. Parents don't seem to give a shit about anything relating to their kids except keeping them at room temperature. They graduated from the School of HVAC Parenting.'

Macy was dying. She was doing that adorable thing where

she was trapped in fits of laughter and each one came out as a prolonged squeak with her gorgeous eyes so full of warmth. All of her features working in concert. I never felt better than when I could make my girls laugh. I thought I was bordering on obnoxious rant but if Macy thought it was hysterical, who was I to argue?

CHAPTER FIVE

Rideau Street, for three or four blocks, is pretty fucked up. The probability of running into someone or something utterly inexplicable is alarmingly high when you walk or even drive down this narrow little thoroughfare. Perhaps the people that inhabit this stretch of Loveland believe it to be normal, if we are playing fast and loose with the barometer that deems things to be north or south of that somewhat abstract term. Ostensibly, it's a weird street.

Daisy murmured gently and jerked a couple of limbs in that inimitable fashion kids and adults alike do when navigating the shallow water immediately before plunging headlong into the abyss of REM or non-REM; I can never remember which is more fathomless.

'I think she needs a booster seat. Did I already say that?' I off-gassed.

'Yes, she does. And I'm not sure. Maybe. I can't remember.'

'Yeah… pretty sure I did. Can't remember either. My long-term's getting as shitty as my short-term… her legs are flailing all over the place in that thing.'

Macy chuckled as she gazed through the protective glass keeping us from touching the weirdness with any sort of tactility.

'She looks like a ventriloquist's dummy.'

She let out a nice big snorty laugh this time and covered her mouth to not wake Daisy. We both shot a glance back at Daisy. Mine through the rear-view; Macy's full-bodied. Daisy did not stir.

'Do you think the people on this street try to be weird as some sort of affectation or do you think they're genuinely abnormal? Either way, I'm cool with it.'

'They're like demented. And deranged.'

I let out a belly laugh and tried to suppress it the best I could. Macy smiled at the horror movie tagline she had just invariably created on the fly.

'Yeah, that they are.'

'No, I mean like they've got serious mental problems. Not like the students. Students are the usual… but the homeless guys. There are average hobos and then these ones.'

We were stuck at a red with dusty fumes all around the car. Pollen and construction haze covered the windshield. Everywhere I looked, I saw stone, jagged rock, holes in the ground begging to turn into sinkholes and workers with orange suits and even more orange skin. Contraband cigarettes dangling from their mouths in cliché fashion with the requisite 'Stop/Slow Down' sign in one hand and a Timmy's Double Double in the other. Rim all rolled up until the next time; if they had a free hand, their fingers would be crossed.

'Do you remember that hobo outside the Metro that one time? Can't remember if it was still Loeb or if they had changed it…'

'It was Metro.'

'Do you remember that guy? We drove by him and he like took a shit right then and there on the sidewalk.'

Macy's eyes widened with such a charming and guileless bent, it put a smile on my face.

'Oh my God! Yes! That was so fucked up!'

'Like he actually took a dump right there on the street.'

'I told you they're mentally ill.'
'Was he a Native?'
'Yeah, I think he was.'
'Am I supposed to say First Nations?'
'Well, it's not supposed to matter at all. You're not even supposed to mention his race.'

My eyes furrowed a bit. I was about to embark on a quick discourse trying to make myself seem like I was the first one to think of this politically correct critique banter when I was actually unequivocally unoriginal. But, maybe not wrong.

'So, I can never mention anyone's race?'
'Right.'
'I can't identify anyone by their race?'
'Yeah.'
'What if I compliment them?'
'Then it's okay.'
'So, I can't say "remember that Native who took a shit in front of the Metro that one time"?'
'The idea is that there's no reason to bring up his race?'
'Right... not even as an identifier?'
'It's sticky.'
'Okay. So, saying Native is bad. Saying Indigenous is bad. Saying First Nations is okay.'
'Right.'
'But I can no longer refer to a person's culture and background to identify them. That Indian guy. That Chinese guy.'
'Right.'

Macy looked bored but was humouring me.

'If somebody referred to me as Brown, I wouldn't give a shit. I'd actually like it. And I encourage it.'
'That's you. Not everybody wants to be identified like that.'

'Yeah, evidently.'

I didn't even know why I was arguing about political correctness. I think I was doing it just to do it. I actually loved political correctness. It was an overly extreme form of flattery towards fringe groups who had been shit on their entire lives. Why not show them some love? I just sometimes took the contrarian view to see what it was like to be an unempathetic white guy. Didn't feel the greatest.

We crawled past the Zesty Market. I had a puzzled look on my face.

'Didn't we just pass a Zesty Market? Are there like two of those on the same block?'

Macy ignored me. She pointed further down towards Parliament Hill.

'Hey check it out. Anti-mask rally.'

'Oh, fantastic. Love those guys. Freedom fighters. Or assholes, take your pick.'

Macy grinned without averting her eyes from the potential melee up top. These rallies had become commonplace in the COVID-era and were more of an irritation than anything else. It was one more reminder that privilege and entitlement could masquerade as social justice.

'Mace, why are you so into that shit? Who cares?'

'I'm not, I'm just looking.'

'You're like intense right now.'

'I'm just counting them.'

'I'll do it for you. White, white, white, white, white, delusional Black guy, white, white, white, white, confused looking Brown guy, white, white, white…'

Macy gave off one of those smiles with a foghorn-sounding grunt while sitting inside a far-off glance.

'What are they doing?'

'Nobody knows. Give them a patio and a Coors Light and they should be good.'

We were just rolling past the Chapters on our right and moved slowly closer to the Mackenzie King Bridge, right over the overpriced haute couture stores on our right and homeless refuge under the bridge on our left.

'Hey, remember that story Carlos told us when we were doing that inventory that one time?'

'Hmm?'

'About the homeless dude who used to melt down shoe polish and dip bread into it for the alcohol content.'

'Oh my God, yes. What the fuck?'

'And the homeless woman who dipped her tampons in alcohol and stuck it up there.'

'Who told you that one? Jesus.'

'It was Carlos when he lived on the streets for a few years. At the Men's Mission.'

'Oh my God. I remember that. I couldn't finish lunch after hearing it.'

'Well, you grew up around Elmvale and Russell projects. That was pretty real right?'

'Not as real as doused tampons.'

I laughed. Maybe a bit louder than I had intended. I felt like an asshole. But, wasn't sure I really was one. I was a decent guy. Refused to give money to the homeless on the streets but instead bought them a Double Double and Timbits. I let seniors go ahead of me in line at the grocery store. I let them have my seat on the bus along with pregnant teenagers and the physically challenged. Or developmentally-delayed. Can't remember what to call them now… I paid it forward. I didn't eat nachos at the movies since they were too crunchy and would make things loud for other patrons.

We veered away from the crazy and towards the NAC on Elgin. Glorious place. Glenn Gould's piano is on display in there. Oscar Peterson is chilling outside. Macy and I got married on the rooftop there two years before Daisy was born. It looks different now. I think it's been renovated. I gestured to Macy over to where we had our nuptials on a classic muggy Ottawa day. She peered over and flashed her sometimes beguiling grin.

'Remember the rain that day?' she muttered.

'I do. It was a blessing. It cooled everything down. Ceremony inside; party outside under the tent. Perfect.'

There was a hum. Almost inaudible but perceptible. I swear I could hear something. Maybe construction far off in the distance.

CHAPTER SIX

When I lived in New York and hopped in a classic yellow cab, I told the immigrant driver (natch) I was going to Christopher Street. He smiled and I had no idea why at the time. Then a few moments passed and he informed me, with no regard for tact whatsoever, that it was home to 'all the fags.'

I returned a neutral 'hmm' and he continued on his way speeding towards red light after red light. It wasn't original to notice how they did that but I was still baffled as to why. Had the tension of driving in a condensed metropolis become so overwhelming that inexplicable acts became normalised?

I saw an old Asian man of maybe about eighty see a car pretty harmlessly go through a yellow light, not even a red, and he took his cane and hammered the side of the already beat-up Honda and yelled out a vocally gnarled 'Fecckkkkkk yuuuuuu!' The city had taken on an almost superficial persona of harried citizens who walk too fast and yell at passing cars who commit even minor infractions. It wasn't that New Yorkers wanted to be aggressive action warriors power-walking up those sidewalks; it's like they felt they had to be. It was weird for me to witness it. That old Chinese dude or wherever the fuck he was from, screaming at a car. So bizarre. Who does that? For what purpose? He had surrendered his identity for the collective ideal of the 'New York Asshole.' I wasn't sure why I was even thinking those things. New York is my favourite city.

Oh yes. The Gay Village on Bank Street here is what made

me think of Christopher Street in Greenwich Village. I was rooming with this Pennsylvania bumpkin at the time. He was a super sweet guy but I was a critical Middle Eastern with a severe superiority complex so it wasn't a great match. He was excited to eat at the Bubba Gump Shrimp Co. in Times Square and I was such an insufferable asshole, I had to shit all over it. I wish I had been nicer. What made me think that wanting to eat at that franchise in glossy 42nd Street made someone lesser? I'm good for some shrimp. I should have taken him up on it instead of shooting him a contemptuous glance. Even if it's twenty per cent shrimp and eighty per cent breading, it would've been worth not killing his dream. Maybe he was Bubba?

I will never forget him walking up to our apartment and telling me that he had seen two guys making out like mad fools outside the Kettle of Fish. His small-town response was awe-inspiring and also his favourite refrain – 'That was a bit overwhelming.' It indeed was. I had seen some of that in Ottawa but nothing to make me seem like an old hand. Everybody wants to appear more authentic than the next, thinking that they've seen all varieties, but two guys kissing had become pretty normal and frankly kind of boring.

The Nissan Rogue was casually skating up Bank Street. A three or four-block stretch that was all gay, all the time.

'Hey, is Invisible Cinema gone?'

'Yeah, they left a few years ago.'

'Remember the guys who owned that place?'

Macy was grinning like an idiotic schoolgirl who just farted in class. I absolutely adored when she had that smug yet burglar's look on her lovely mug.

'Yeah, I remember them. What about them?'

'They wanted to fuck you.'

I smiled and stared all around me. Bank Street was covered with cars, bikers, pedestrians, parked cars, and buses who would rather crush you in that little accordion bit in the middle than let you pass them. Not yielding to an OC Transpo was a strangely punishable offence. Like those lunatic drivers couldn't yield to us for a change. If I've already committed, maybe slow down so you don't annihilate me. Just a thought.

'Yeah, I think you're a little off the mark on that one. Flattering for sure. But, not likely.'

'They flirted with you all the time.'

'We just talked movies. They really knew their shit. They had like every DVD you could think of.'

'Remember when they called you about your credit card?'

'What about it? I forgot my credit card and they called me so I could go there and pick it up.'

'Whatever. One of them rode on a motorised scooter and the other was always eyeing you. And you talked about his T-shirt.'

'Yeah, he had a Vestron Video T-shirt on. I thought it was funny. I remember Vestron from when I was a kid. They made all kinds of shitty films that I bought posters for.'

'They thought you were gay. So did I when I met you.'

Macy laughed one of those abrupt guttural cries that didn't sound like anything except an involuntary spasm. I loved when she did that as well. I always felt I had achieved something. But, she was laughing at her own joke so whatever.

'I thought you were a lesbian so who gives a shit.'

'No, you didn't, shut the fuck up.'

'No, I didn't. True... you're not the first girl who thought I was a fag.'

'Queer.'

'Yeah, what is that about? Why is "queer" the proper term for gay people? Why would they want a word that inherently means "weird" as their identifier? I'd rather be called a fag, to be honest. Who the fuck wants to be called queer? It's like you're defining yourself as weird when you're not.'

'You're saying that stuff like you're the first person to have ever thought of it.'

'So, because it's not original, it's not worth saying. Okay. That makes a lot of sense.'

'Just keep it down a bit. Daisy's stirring.'

'Stirring? Who says that any more?'

'Yeah, I'm not sure where that came from.'

This street had been the spot for many a Gay Pride Parade over the years. They'd shut down the whole street and it would be a joyous free for all of feather boas, make-up, 70s disco tunes, neon speedos and gas masks. It was great family entertainment.

Macy and I loved the gay community and had several gay friends so because we met that quota, we felt that we could sporadically give our opinions about gay culture without fear of reprisal. We had a couple of social justice warrior gay friends and there was not one thing we could say that was critical in even a minor key without them losing their shit all over us.

Macy just said, 'What's with the gas masks and leather and sexual imagery?'

It was a valid point. Yes, celebrate your culture and enjoy your newly burgeoning and long overdue freedom. But, is it totally appropriate to grind on each other with gas masks and dildos in the middle of a sleepy Ottawa afternoon with blue-collar worker bees enjoying their obligatory patio Coors Light?

Thinking about it made me bored. The quotidian stimulus-response of humdrum Ottawa life. It put me in a furiously aggressive sense of fatigue. Everywhere I looked, I didn't see faces and places; I saw opinions waiting to be heard. Lofty declarations and trite recriminations. Was the rest of the world like Ottawa?

CHAPTER SEVEN

Macy was two weeks away from her due date with Daisy and we had been driving the, at that time, fairly new Rogue. We had joined the vapid clan of SUV owners to my chagrin. But, I put the chagrin away and decided that it was the correct decision as it was safer than any other vehicle that was remotely appropriate.

We were driving up Old Ottawa South, past Stella Luna's Gelato classics. It was a place Macy and I had gone to several times that served designer sweets. Kind of like going to Oh So Good in the ByWard Market where you can buy a $15 piece of chocolate cake and somehow justify it. Here at least, the gelato didn't cost you a psychotically exorbitant amount. We hadn't been to Stella Luna even once without a classic Glebe-ite standing at the counter telling their life story, introducing their dog, explaining the many varied breeds of dog that made up this particular dog, and of course asking to 'test' the different flavours of gelato, one by excruciating one.

It was these moments that I wished the owners would pull a Marco Pierre White and tell ignorant and inconsiderate patrons like this to fuck off and not come back. But, Ottawa folk don't react that way. They put their thumbs up their asses and take it with glee. Yes, of course, ma'am, how many more of our selection would you like to try? You've tried all the gelato and sorbet; why not have a sample of our latest quiches and tourtieres?

It's weird though. When Daisy was three, we went to Stella

Luna all the time. We'd all get smalls because anything larger was like eating a goddamn tub of ice cream. And with the overhang, you get enough all right. I'd always get hazelnut or pistachio; absolutely glorious ice cream. Macy would get a bizarre combination of gelato and sorbet which always sounded sickly to me. Rich chocolate gelato with a lime sorbet? What the hell was that? And Daisy would always opt for either French vanilla or lemon sorbet.

We'd sit by the window in the big comfy chairs, and play I Spy while we watched the OC Transpo buses barrel down Bank Street watching Birkenstock after Birkenstock. Man-bun after man-bun. Dog after dog after goddamn dog. Snow piles pushed against the sidewalk covered in dogshit and dog piss. A vomit-inducing array of rum-raisin designs all over the freshly fallen white stuff. But, it's okay I guess. We don't want to offend the dogs and their dedicated dog owners. Why should it bother us when animals use snowbanks as their personal bathrooms? I love going for a walk with my family and seeing how many shit pellets I can count and how many marmalade smears I can spot, if I'm not stepping on them outright. Don't want to hurt the feelings of all those pug-shih-tzu-malamute-bernese and whatever the fuck else concoctions.

When Macy and I, sans Daisy at the time, kept sauntering up Bank Street more directly into the Glebe, we first hit Lansdowne. The Glebe existed in a wonderful little antique shop curio sort of shell. It was untouched and untouchable. Until the Lansdowne crew came and created a gargantuan behemoth of pomp and circumstance right at the foot of the Glebe, the bridge and then Old Ottawa South.

Lansdowne was an attempt to bring more revenue and attention to the area and it certainly did that, unfortunately, at the expense of the smaller mom-and-pop shops in the area. So many small businesses went under but it was just the price of 'competition' and 'growth'. I always loved the Glebe for its narrowness, uniqueness and sheer obnoxiousness. Little shops that sold wonderful things for absurd prices. Places you could window-shop at and maybe buy something from once a year. I was comfortable with its haughty aspirations.

Then Lansdowne comes in as a complete non-sequitur. A gigantic stadium, a multiplex movie theatre with actual dinner service and drinks (like it's adhering to the blueprint of dinner theatre where a bunch of senile octogenarians will attempt to watch an O'Neill play through their bifocals while eating minute steak and powdered potatoes with condensed milk; except the new model has no irony whatsoever), restaurants that are so antiseptic they look like business offices, and of course the hooking-up scene. There were two restaurants there – Joey and Local – and I finally realised they were actually two different restaurants. They seemed like ideal Tinder destinations. They were super grimy and super fratty. It was like a Chad or Brock bomb had exploded in those two joints.

So, as our intrepid Rogue went up Bank Street, we were in front of a music repair shop of some kind waiting at a red light. There was some buffer between us and the car in front of us. A car decides to cut out of the Rogers parking lot quickly between us and the other car to dart across to the opposite lane. But, the second they darted, they hit the exact moment a car was coming their way and crunched the shit out of their car and the colliding party.

They side-swiped our now sad little Rogue, while getting totalled and totalling the car they were in the way of, and also slammed into a parked car that had a mother and four-year-old boy in it, taking out a lamppost for good measure.

The drivers had Quebec licence plates. I didn't really give a shit about stereotyping. As a Brown guy, I had heard it all and didn't care. I was always happy to report that every Quebec driver I had ever seen drove like they had been hit with a taser up their assholes. Something about being in the driver's seat turned them into enraged, frothy ghouls who would seem perfectly at home in a violent dystopian future where gasoline was at a premium. Why were they so amped behind the wheel? So angry. It's like they didn't want to be late for the Habs game so they could complain about all the non-calls every twenty seconds.

The driver of the colliding car was geriatric, so he didn't really know what to make of all this except that his front fender had been warped to shit, and he didn't have any words. The offending party was a twenty-something Quebecker kid with a mechanic's hat (shocker) and a flannel shirt (double shocker). He had a dopey look on his face like he thought, again, that we were at a Habs game and this was some big misunderstanding. Why did he just get tossed out of the game?

He looked incredulous and the lady whose parked car he slammed into was screaming at him. I remember her saying, 'You drove across that street like a bat out of hell!' That was such an Ottawa thing to say. Her young son, despite his tears, was all right, thank goodness. By the grace of some mysterious deity, he was okay. I would always have been grateful for the safety of everyone but something about my impending fatherhood made me feel especially relieved that that poor kid was okay. They had camping equipment in the back and I overheard him asking his mother if they were still going camping. She said, 'Well we can't after this! We have to take our car in.' I felt awful for them. Their weekend trip was shot and the poor kid was justifiably crying disappointed tears because of this piece of shit irresponsible asshole who took a moronic and totally uncalled-for chance thunder bolting between two cars into oncoming traffic.

Macy was the best though. We were fine but we were going to go to the doctor anyway to make sure the shock of the events didn't affect her and our unborn child in any way. It was cumbersome to do but definitely necessary. We wanted to be sure Daisy was okay.

Macy got out of the car and started screaming in this prick's face. It was glorious. 'What the fuck is the matter with you? You could have killed somebody? I'm pregnant and I could have lost the baby!'

It was a classic example of Macy having balls and me having none. I think it was Virginia Woolf, or someone like that I'm not sure, who said, and I'm paraphrasing, that the most interesting couples are the ones in which the male is more feminine and the female is more masculine. I think that qualified us as being interesting.

I stood by with a goofy grin on my maw as Macy laid into this sucker. The kid had the balls to come back with, 'Well obviously I made a mistake!' Macy looked at me and I gave her the non-verbal 'proceed' signal. The fireworks continued and more Glebe-ites stopped to see what was happening. There were no snowbanks since this was August so their dogs were taking Niagara Falls pisses all over the electrical poles that were already gnarled up from all the posters and staples embedded deep in the wood. Those dogs have to mark their territory in the Glebe. Don't want any open mic night musicians or boho buskers infringing on their space.

In all the sweaty bluster of this traffic incident and subsequent histrionics, I decided to chime in with a 'Dude, what the fuck is the matter with you?' Macy was glad I had joined in and the Quebecker kid looked defeated now that a belligerent Brown guy was in his face. Then, wouldn't you know it, a knobby-kneed guy who must've been in his fifties saunters up to me and says, 'Maybe you should shut up.'

I looked at him and said, 'What? This guy just crashed his car and could've hurt somebody including my wife who's pregnant.'

The guy says, 'There are two sides to every story.'

I was so flabbergasted by this exchange, I actually, in classic Ottawa fashion, said nothing more and took it right up the ass. I was thinking of what things I should say. a) There are no sides to this story. This driver was irresponsible and almost caused deaths; b) I am angry because he almost hurt us and our unborn child; c) What fucking business is this of yours anyway! Go on with your life. What are you stopping here for anyway?

I stood there and couldn't summon the courage to give him any of these New York answers. I went with an Ottawa answer instead: 'What breed of dog is that anyway?'

As the knobby-kneed asshole licked his lips ready to spout the 'humane society/pure breed/stray dog/rescue/canine miracle/fifty breeds in one' anecdote that all dog owners think is unique, I stared down at the pavement, which was covered in dog urine, cracked asphalt and splintered car parts and mournfully swallowed.

CHAPTER EIGHT

How did I find myself back on Rideau Street? Macy had nodded off again, poor thing. I was always in the habit of asking her where we were despite my having been an Ottawa resident since I was seven years old. Without her navigational skills, I'd probably find myself somewhere outside the city limits in the nether regions of Renfrew or Pembroke.

We buggered up Rideau Street again and the flash of familiarity hit me again. The poverty and overt sense of defiance.

To my right was the ByTowne Cinema. The infernal pestilence of COVID had turned most cities into a Ferris wheel of lockdowns but some small businesses got slapped a bit harder, in the ByTowne's case, folding into submission. I heard on Hot 89.9 from that overly chatty morning crew that the cinema would be closing. I had never felt such crushing melancholy for the closure of a building. In its most reductive sense, I was mourning a pile of bricks. The corner of Rideau and Nelson. The steeple of cinema for Ottawa residents who actually wanted to see something outside the arcade-riddled theme parks all over the suburbs from Kanata to Orleans.

I always made a habit of getting there a bit before showtime because I wanted to pop into the used bookstore next door. It was such a wonderfully cliché hipster bookstore replete with coming-apart carpeting, proud disorganisation and gloriously musty-stink books piled wherever you could look. If there was a bathroom in there, you wouldn't be short of reading material, likely on the floor and on top of the toilet bowl. This was the kind of joint where the owner would consistently get the following query, 'Do you have any David Foster Wallace?'

Walking into the ByTowne was kind of like stepping into a grindhouse cinema in Los Angeles but much less belligerent and quite a bit cleaner. It had random carpeting here and there with no real sense of cohesion. Some posters on the walls, kind of peeling, and some others in bins that you could buy for a small fee. A tight, tight, tight bathroom which had two doors leading into it for some inexplicable reason, like you were going to urinate in an inner sanctum of some kind. A very buttery-smelling popcorn station on the way in. Flyers for local art festivals before you made your way to your seat. Cracked floors here and there.

Somebody who had actually been to a grindhouse cinema (not me) might visit the ByTowne and think it was the swankiest picture house they'd ever visited. But for me, compared to the comfy chair treatment of the latest multiplexes, this place was endearingly scuzzy. I loved its sense of polite grime.

Once when I needed to piss in an awful way, I had no choice but to use the wheelchair-accessible stall in the bathroom. There were three urinals I believe and two stalls (one regular and one wheelchair). Even though the urinals were free, I didn't use them. What people found normal about urinals, I never did. Maybe it was growing up as a Brown guy in an immigrant household, but the notion of urinating directly adjacent to other male strangers and then 'cleaning' yourself by wiggling your penis around a little porcelain bowl, and then tucking said pee-dribbled penis back in your boxer-briefs didn't exactly smell like home.

So, I would always pee in stalls but the regular one was in use, so I used the wheelchair one. When has a dude in a wheelchair ever rolled up and started to bang on the stall door because someone's in there. I don't think I've ever seen a wheelchair anywhere within spitting distance of one of those stalls before. But, I decide to take a piss in one and a guy knocks on the door. My heart felt like it stopped beating. I was in a serious ethical breach. I did something you are not to do. I told him, "Coming."

I walked out and saw his piercing eyes. Not pleased. In another city, I would probably have been dealt with some serious wheelchair road rage but, in Ottawa, that steely glare was enough to mean he would try to roll over me if given the chance. But it was Ottawa. I am sure he would hold back and he did.

I quickly used those sad little sinks where you have to use one hand to wash and one hand to repeatedly turn the faucet on and off, as it shuts off after two seconds of use. Using ByTowne hand-washing stations is like giving your hands a mini-Baptism over and over again with some pink granular soap. My hands were still soapy and I wanted to get the hell out of there.

The wheelchair guy was now safely ensconced in his stall and had no bashfulness whatsoever to fart as loudly as possible in there. Another thing I always had a hard time understanding in these public washrooms. Don't people feel like they should have a sense of mini decorum? Maybe fart a little less loudly? Let it out one spurt at a time so the entire washroom doesn't hear something so patently disgusting? Maybe hit the flush right when you drop everything so others don't have to hear that vile 'plop plop' sound? But this was coming from a guy who blatantly used a wheelchair stall just so I didn't have to swing my dick in front of other men at the urinals. I guess my sense of moral duty and paying it forward had some strange shadings.

I ran out of that washroom and found my usual seat, close to the front but directly to the left or right, whichever was emptiest.

My biggest worry was that wheelchair guy was going to complain to the owner and staff about what I did in the bathroom and that I'd be banned from the ByTowne for life. It wasn't any moral quandary that was bothering me. I just wanted to be able to keep coming here. Please don't take this place from me, wheelchair guy. This is my favourite Ottawa spot. I need this place.

I remember after seeing a film here and being so mesmerised, on a hot Saturday afternoon, that I went out and sat on the bench outside the Loblaws, which was usually reserved for exceptionally loud hobos, and perched there and enjoyed the baby blue sky.

During the final fifteen minutes of one very intense film, you could not hear a single sound in the place. That kind of hypnotised communion that was your average night at this cinema. I mean dead silence like being at the top of the Tyrolean mountains and not even being able to hear air.

I was once in line on a semi-snowy Saturday night and the queue was around the block, past the Mac's convenience store, and the other line (for ticket buyers, not holders, I forget which was which), went past that other building, which I think was a hotel. An older lady in line, with some pretty heavy foundation on her cheeks, asked me, 'Are there this many people here because the film won the Palme d'Or or because it's just a Saturday night?'

I answered, 'Probably the second one.'

I gave an obnoxiously arch smile and she replied with, 'But I have heard that this film is supposed to be one of the best of the decade.'

I felt I had offended her by my shitty smug style so I tried to repent with, 'Is that right? I hope it's amazing. I'm looking forward to seeing it. Where did you find out about it? Are you excited?' Maybe I had laid on the repentance a bit thick. She didn't say much and turned around. Guess I whiffed on that one.

I was utterly blown by that marvellous film when it was done and when the credits rolled, there was some awkward applause here and there, and then one guy yelled, 'Boooooo!' I had never seen that kind of Tourettes-ish response at the end of a film here before. I was half annoyed because I loved the film so much and half amused by this display of seemingly arbitrary emotion. I think this guy maybe thought he was actually at the Cannes Film Festival, and not the corner of Rideau and Nelson, where it smells like butter and pee in equal measure when you exit. Where do people summon up the courage to express such a defiant opinion so openly and publicly? Kudos to that guy even if he appeared to be a potential future tenant of the Royal Ottawa Mental Health Centre/Home for the Criminally Whacked-Out.

Seeing a martial arts film there was the closest the ByTowne ever got to an actual concert. It was the middle of the Christmas holidays so everyone's boots, that were initially caked with dirty snow, were now inelegantly melting on all of those cracked floors, and the black and brown liquid residue was seeping down all directions, creating little pools of filth, aided in design by the many fractures in the floor. The place had a buzzing sound that I wasn't used to hearing there because every single seat was filled. And after each fight scene, while the audience was held rapt, they started cheering like lunatics, admiring the artistry. It was unique to see a crowd like that there. I loved that shift in gears.

Once, there was a documentary that was fifteen hours and, you could buy a special pass, that would give you a discount and would allow you entry at any of its showings that you preferred. I went through the whole process and found an amazing kinship with the crowd I had never felt before. I started recognising the faces as they continued showing up. It was the same bunch of people I'd see, in addition to the one-offs who wanted to see a part here or part there. None of us spoke with one another. We just acknowledged each other, like the head bob you'd give to other kids in high school when you'd pass them in the halls but didn't really want to talk with them. By the end of the documentary, the owner of the ByTowne came to the front and thanked us all for coming out. For loving cinema like that. It was so lovely. It didn't feel like something that would happen at a multiplex. I couldn't picture the pimply git teenager who rips your ticket to come in and address the audience after a show with a keynote speech. He's probably anxious to go home and jerk off. If he didn't already do it on his break in the cinema stalls.

For God's sake, wheelchair guy, don't ban me for life from this place. The Proustian smack I'd feel every time I'd walk into that cinema was indelible. That semi-dirty semi-sanitised stink of the urinal cakes in the bathroom was the equivalent of a madeleine cake.

The blessing was that I heard, again on Hot 89.9 (I think) that the ByTowne was going to be saved. This altar was going to be absolved from ruin, from the stench, from the disease of COVID. It wasn't going to smash this place down. It fell upon hard times, went under and then was sold to some new freshies. It stands tall, thank God. And I wasn't banned, thank you, wheelchair guy. I had a hankering to go to the Horn of Africa, an Ethiopian restaurant across the street but it was closed. I heard it was shut down, but not by the scourge of COVID. I think this may have been a health code violation. So it goes.

CHAPTER NINE

Daisy's head gently kissed the side of her booster seat headrest. She was as fresh as Mexican cocaine. I just wanted to put that powder on a shard of grimy glass, segment that snow into generous portions and fucking snort her up, up, up and away. Daisy had no impurities; no defects. No residue or mould. She was, and by God's grace would always be, here now.

I glanced at her in the rear-view over and over. My head stayed static while my eyeballs shifted to mirror and in front, mirror and in front. I was so enamoured by her gorgeous lashes, flickering while the A/C vent's fumes softly wafted onto her. The SUV was the tacky upgrade from the horror of the mini-van. It made suburbanites like us feel like we didn't live in the suburbs when we actually did. We wanted to live in the Glebe with all those pseudo-intellectual granola assholes but the houses were goddamn money pits. Was it really worth it to us to spend God knows what to buy a Glebe home and then double it just to fix the plumbing and furnace that only functioned circa pre-war? As much as we yearned to *walk* to the farmer's market instead of having to drive there and park underground Lansdowne like all the 'outsiders', living in a house that was either as modern as fuck or as decrepit as one built for returning veterans didn't seem like a viable or desirable option.

But, Daisy. But, Daisy... the glory of your cheek, kid. I felt like a cliché-riddled prick but to see a child in the throes of sleep. Ravished by their own serenity. It was the stuff that dreams were made of. I wonder where her mind is. Is she drifting in limbo or actually visualising something? My eyelids were becoming seriously fatigued by the back and forth; I was getting worried I was staring at her more than the car in front of me. All we needed was dealing with some Karen in a Lexus mad that her flash shit box got a minor ding in the fender. If that Karen puts her finger in my face, I'll bite it off and feed it to my kid.

'What's with your eyes?'

Macy rejoined the voyage, with the usual sequence of mild grunts, eyes flickering, crusty eyes and mouth and incoherent gibberish on entry. It would be so refreshing to see somebody wake up from sleep with a jolt and a 'how do you do' without any lag time. A rise and a jump just for the sake of novelty.

'You're back. You were snoring.'

'No, I wasn't.'

'Why does everybody deny snoring like it's a sin? Everybody snores. Who gives a shit?'

'God, you're salty.'

'I'm not salty. Funny Face is still sleeping PS.'

'You just driving around?'

'Looks that way. You missed Horn of Africa.'

'I think they closed it down.'

'Yeah, the place looked boarded up… well, it kinda looked boarded up even when it was open so all good, I guess.'

Macy offered a post-nap chuckle, which is really like a hearty belly laugh in ordinary circumstances so I considered that a win.

'Did I ever tell you about when I went there with my family for my birthday one year?'

'No.' Macy smiled in anticipation of where this was going.

'They all sit down and immediately, in classic Iranian

fashion, sneer at the décor, sneer at the tablecloth which was really just plastic, sneer at the cutlery, sneer at the Injera bread, which they declared out loud was not actually bread—'

Macy howled with laughter and I grimaced. Happy for the laugh but worried it might wake up Daisy.

'She's out, Darius, don't worry.'

'Okay... so yeah they just shit on the entire place. And the idea of eating with their hands didn't exactly go over well. And they were so overdressed. Dad was wearing a suit. Like, what the fuck? There were Ottawa U guys in there in flip-flops. Middle Eastern men always have to wear a suit to restaurants. It's Ottawa. Everybody dresses like shit. No formality needed.'

I could sense Macy was done with my ranting so she changed the subject.

'Are we in Vanier?'

'Yeah. Approaching.'

Every city has a region that is stereotypically known as a forgotten netherworld. It reeks of poverty and lack of opportunity. Little ghettos that are the sickly cousins of adjacent and flourishing neighbourhoods. Ottawa was that rare bird that dispersed these unfortunate and sad districts all over the entire city, from Orleans (down the hill of course) to Bayshore (pick a Mid-East resto that had shootings).

Vanier was the godfather of shit. The reek of Ottawa. The leper colony in the midst of the general Ottawa mediocrity. Residents of Vanier would probably hear that and cry foul but, if given the chance to live anywhere else, they would move without hesitation; all bang and no whimper. 'How dare you speak about our neighbourhood like that?' Shut the fuck up. I lived in the housing co-op apartments near Elmvale which, late one unfortunate night while we were all sleeping, had an 'honour killing' right across the street in the Loblaws parking lot so I knew a thing or two about fucked up areas. Believe me when I say anyone would rather move out of those cesspools than stay. Nobody is saying to move to Rothwell Heights or Rockcliffe Park or other obnoxiously snooty gated communities. But, preferably something without daily stabbings for leisure.

But, Vanier. Jesus, sweet Jesus, Vanier. I had a friend come from Toronto who thought that Vanier was worse than Jane and Finch. He said he could handle the gang violence of Jane and Finch since, if you stayed out of their way, they had no beef with you. Vanier, however, made you a part of its world when you entered.

I caught out of the corner of my eye the Shoppers Drug Mart that used to be the old Vanier cinema. $4.25 on any night but $2.50 on Tuesday nights for old runs. It had rock-hard seats and had salons the size of your living room which created an odd viewing experience; as if you invited complete strangers to your home for a movie night. I remember watching a movie and not really enjoying it at all. It was restricted but somehow this young Asian kid got in, slightly androgynous, and sucked down his Coca-Cola and then proceeded to suck on the ice cubes. On top of that, the HVAC system was so loud there were whole patches of dialogue you couldn't even hear. Nobody seemed to care since they had paid so little to get in. Everything came down to value for money.

Across the street, I spied the Haitian Creole restaurant.

'Oh my God, the Haitian place is closed!'

Macy looked genuinely despondent. I shared her sentiment. Another small business done in by the VID. The Haitian place was classic islands vibes. Goat and Riz Djon Djon. Dirty rice. Pikliz. I adored that place; we had catering from there for Daisy's third birthday. We had the family over and received the obligatory Iranian sneers when presented with something slightly off the highway. That goat though. So pungent in the best possible way.

Sitting in the Haitian restaurant waiting for the catering order to be filled was the typical islands experience. A few gentlemen sitting at a beat-up old teak table playing dominos and eating oxtail soup. A fan kinda sorta working, blowing what felt like a hot wind in my face, if that was possible. A television from the 1980s somehow still operational playing music videos from the old country. And the head cook/owner/waitress/cashier looking at me as if she had no idea what I was doing in there.

I let her know I was waiting for my order which had been placed the day before. She nodded in what appeared to be comprehension but then remained stationary. I didn't hear anyone in the back so I assumed she was the head chef. I was waiting for the order but didn't understand what this interaction was exactly. The MO of a place like this was different from the norm; not about turnover but employer relaxation and subsequent customer confusion. I waited for ten minutes on a sturdy stool, while my underwear became moist, and stared out the window at the freaks outside.

There were grown men on BMX bikes. And even more grown men on skateboards. Obese women sauntered down the street with a stroller and three other kids in tow; four kids in total. Then a meth-head couple screaming at each other about who cheated on who, while they also pushed a stroller. Good grief.

Crack whores everywhere. I didn't want to generalise and put all prostitutes into one bin. Some, I am sure, are crack whores but others meth whores, and some maybe just enjoy fucking for money. But, the look of some of them set my teeth on edge and made my heart sink into a profound melancholy that lasted for about five seconds and then I was wondering what was happening with my order.

I didn't want to be the guy who didn't 'get' the vibe of the place, screeching, 'Where's my food? I've been waiting?' I looked over and finally saw the cashier move to the back. My heart leapt. Get cooking for fuck's sake; we have a birthday party to start.

I looked out the window and again saw belligerence. Was it a Vanier quota that had to be met to have someone every ten minutes say or do something offensive, impolite or overtly aggressive? A guy walked across the street into oncoming traffic, cars honked at him to move out of the way, and he told them to 'fuck off' and gave them the finger. What exactly was the intention of this exchange? What was meant to be accomplished? I was convinced that there was no actual purpose. It was simply a consistently bizarre interaction in Vanier that was all about the weirdness barometer; making sure the checklist was hit for the day. Living in Vanier was not a passive experience; you had to take part in the muck to be the muck.

By some sort of enchanted conjuring, the cashier walked out of the back kitchen while I exited my reverie. She had bags of perfectly packed-up food, steaming and ready to go. She hadn't forgotten about me. I don't know why I doubted her. At that moment, I wanted to kiss her and thank her for making this glorious food with so much love. How did she get all this ready and cooked so quickly? It smelled so magnificent, I wanted to partake then and there but first needed to figure out how to get all of this from here to the car without having a close encounter with some crazies. I thanked the lady heartily and I gave a twenty-five per cent tip. She gave me an extra crispy fried fish appetiser. I wanted to stay and keep exchanging gifts with this lady but I had to dash.

My wallet bulged out of my right shorts pocket and my cell made a slightly less pronounced one in my left; my shorts looked like they were on steroids. I had to remember to not put my phone in my pocket right next to my balls. The phone felt hot and my balls pulsed next to them. It all felt very gross.

On my way to the car, I saw a hobo outside a diner. I jetted to the car, put the food in the front seat with no worry that it would get cold since it was thirty-five degrees Celsius outside. I hurried back to where the hobo was and saw a sixty-year-old-ish man with tanned skin to the point of imported leather. This guy was browner than I was but white as baking soda in his original model.

'Dude, are you okay?'

'Do you have any spare change?'

'I don't. Do you want something to eat? Drink?'

'No, just money if you have it.'

'I don't have money. You want some Timmy's? How about a Double Double? Timbits?'

'Yeah okay.'

'Any Timbits you want?'

I was backing away as he was specifying which Timbits but the traffic noise drowned him out. He was still talking so this guy seemed really particular about which Timbits he ate; picky eater I suppose. I figured instead of getting him to repeat it, I'd just get the mixed one. I'd be covered either way.

After finally getting out of the ubiquitous Timmy's lineup, I came back and gave him his coffee and doughnut holes. He took them and didn't say anything. He started drinking the coffee and I didn't wait around to see his reaction to the Timbits in case I got his directions all wrong.

I hopped in the car and drove off. Inching closer to the Vanier limits, I wondered if I'd get there without something bizarre happening or a pedestrian yelling at a passing car. There was time.

CHAPTER TEN

'What's this all about?' I said with a degree of alertness.

'Looks like an accident. Shit, the whole front of that Mini Cooper is torn off.'

'My goodness… why's that cop giving the tow truck driver a ticket?'

'Because he's too close.'

'What does that mean?'

'At an accident, the tow truck driver's only supposed to be a certain number of feet away and can't be any closer.'

'Huh?'

'They can tap into police frequencies and they can hear whenever there's an accident so they drive over and they're supposed to be far enough away.'

I was utterly baffled that I knew none of this. My ignorance in so many matters was astounding. Macy was so knowledgeable about so many things in the quotidian realm.

'So, when somebody gets into an accident, the cops come and then when they need a tow truck driver, they won't need to call one because there's one sitting right there?'

'Right.'

'But why the fuck does a tow truck driver have access to police airwaves? Isn't that like private?'

'Not sure.'

'How grimy is that? Jesus… a bunch of these asshole tow truck drivers tap into signals they're not supposed to and just park their trucks a few feet away from grisly accidents?'

'Right.'

'Am I the only one who thinks that's messy? Isn't it illegal to tap into the goddamn police department's frequency?'

The moment that I was beginning to bore Macy with my incessant questions about this, two rival tow truck drivers raced past us with psychotic speed. My jaw clenched with serious discomfort.

'What the fuck is that?'

Macy grabbed the overhanging extension located at the top of the passenger side window. I never thought these were for anything other than hanging a suit if you needed to but apparently, Macy loved to hang onto them, like she was holding a bar to steady herself on a bus or subway, to save her if the car ever crashed. Not sure how that would save her except for leaving her severed arm hanging in place while the rest of her body went flying in the other direction but who was I to tell people how to feel comfortable?

She blurted out with panic, 'Those two tow trucks are trying to get to the scene of that crash. They must've got the signal too and they're competing!'

'But they almost crashed into like two cars and made that other one veer off the road! Don't they give a shit?'

Darius loved humanity. He loved life. If asked whether he could live forever, his answer was invariably yes. Others looked upon immortality as a curse but for him, the notion of actually dying was not only more terrifying than anything one could imagine in fiction, it was also completely repugnant. There were just too many things to do, and read, and watch, and listen to, and too many lovely naps to take, and kisses to partake in, and mornings to cuddle with Macy and Daisy on a Saturday morning in the too-small queen-sized bed, and cups of black coffee to drink with apricot jam on toast, and eggs benedict to eat once a year, and bike riding to do when his ass wasn't developing haemorrhoids from the seat, and strolls through the farmer's market to get fresh greens, and, and, and, and. There were never enough hours in the day to do everything he wanted to do but he concluded that that was a perfect problem to have in this life.

Walking through Lansdowne and seeing so many people sitting on patios and laughing and eating under the hot sun filled him with something more intense than hope. He felt like saying 'esperanza' to render it more potent. Months upon months of COVID lockdowns had bled humanity dry but here were people again living as they had before. He could feel his insides cleansed by the relief of this picture.

But... as much as Darius loved life and all the silliness that resided in Ottawa, the city that he loved and despised equally, at that moment, he wanted the world to end.

The sight of those tow truck drivers flying down the road like Formula One drivers, endangering everyone around them and bullying others off the road, not to mention the overt callousness of spying on police airwaves in order to get to the scene of a potentially horrific accident earlier than others so they could make a quick buck... something about it was so essentially evil, he could not take it.

He understood that these guys were blue-collar workers and needed to make a living like anyone else but something about it felt relentlessly dirty. One could use the obvious rebuttal and declare that there were far more heinous things to become outraged about. Darius understood this. He wasn't stupid. He marvelled at how people would say things that they thought were being uttered for the first time. Like the recipient of this information had apparently never considered this before.

Yes, no one was saying that the habits of tow truck drivers was down in the dumps in league with geo-political evil or serial killers or non-mask-wearing anti-vaxxers. But, something about this ordeal hurt Darius at that moment.

He wished to die at that moment. He could hear death whisper in his ear but for that nanosecond, it didn't bother him like it usually did when he heard it. It always filled him with terror and he immediately attempted to dodge the hot air but this time, he felt a kind of relief and wanted to succumb to the void.

He wanted the world to be enveloped by a giant inescapable tsunami. To take all the evildoers and bastard tow truck drivers away. But, to take them away, we'd all have to be taken away too. To get rid of the cancerous cells with an aggressive chemo, you have to sacrifice the healthy cells as well. For the world to end… but not in a hateful way.

Darius didn't hate the world. He just wanted everyone to do better and be better. Everything he felt people could be, they never were. Why couldn't people be more empathetic? Why didn't they act nobly? Why didn't they put in everything they could for their wives and children?

Darius, before he became a father, got some advice from a close friend of his. His friend said, 'This should become your mantra as a parent – never under any circumstances, yell at your child. Do not scream, don't shout, barely raise your voice. Show infinite patience and respect them and they will in turn respect you.'

Darius felt that it sounded absurd. How was it possible to reason with an infant who hadn't developed fully yet. Surely, it was acceptable to yell now and then? After becoming a father, he realised that this mantra was not only true, but also unused by ninety-nine per cent of parents, and also one that changed his life for the better.

To show unending love and engagement to your child. To show them patience and understanding. To actually *want* to be a parent. Choosing to be a parent not to fulfil some miserable socially induced bucket list but to actually feel that being a parent is something you must do; not obliged to do.

When Darius saw others parenting their kids, he wanted to puke. The Baby Boomers were godawful parents and that, he felt, was universally acknowledged. They were abusive, unresponsive, unempathetic and generally complete assholes. Gen-X parents were a lot like the boomers but exercised a better sense of style; but were ostensibly the same careless pricks that came before them. Gen-Y or Millennial parents were a bit better but still needed lots of work. They at least looked into the reality of seeing a child as a living breathing human being with agency and insight as opposed to a piece of clay that was there to shape into a prima ballerina to be starved day and night. Or forced to play hockey until the requisite athletic scholarship was attained.

But all around him, Darius saw a pandemic. The pandemic wasn't what everyone thought, however. It had been going on years before COVID ever existed. It was bad parenting. The pandemic that would destroy the world wasn't greed or capitalism or disease or the bloody obvious. It was parents who didn't give a shit about being good parents. Or who were just no good at it to begin with. The world over, generations of kids neglected... tossed aside. To grow into what? Well-adjusted and empathetic people? Impossible.

'There is a world elsewhere,' Darius thought. It was from a Shakespeare play he couldn't remember the name of. What could it be? More evolved? More generous souls? Or more of the same?

He just knew that in that one fleeting moment, he wanted to die and wished the world was swallowed, enveloped, annihilated. We could do better, he kept thinking.

Macy nudged me for a second while we were at a red light.

'You good?'

He immediately responded, jumping out of his mini reverie.

'Yeah good. I'm good. Missy still asleep?'

'Yeah.'

'You got one of her granola bars or anything?'

'No, she ate them all.'

'I'm not hungry. I just feel my breath smells.'

'It does.'

'Do you have any of that gum? That gum with no aspartame?'

'Yeah, I do, one second.'

'No actually, forget it. Every time I chew gum, my jaw hurts.'

'You want some water instead.'

'Yes, please. Thanks love.'

CHAPTER ELEVEN

'Can we pass my old house?'

'Sure.'

'Is that okay?'

'Yeah,' I said indifferently but it may have come out wrong when mingled with the quizzical expression I put out there. Not sure why I did that. I don't think any combination of indifference and bafflement would be a good look anyway.

'I still miss Elmvale.'

'Seriously?'

'Well yeah. It was close to downtown and I grew up there. I went to Vincent Massey where every second kid was named Abdi or Mohammed.'

I laughed. 'Yeah, we had no shortage of Brown guys at Gloucester High as well. Excluding me.'

'And Hillcrest was the same.'

'They revamped that place pretty hard though. It's got like this brand-new soccer field. We never had anything that nice. Gloucester was a shithole. Probably still is.'

'It's right next to Jasmine.'

'Yeah, I remember, believe me.'

Macy grew up in Elmvale with her grandma and her little knotted dog. First, we met at a part-time job we both worked at while we were students at Ottawa U and Algonquin. We became fast friends. My parents moved away so I was on my own for the first time so decided to get an apartment in Elmvale to be close to Macy. She let me park my car in her laneway.

When my parents were gone overseas and after my mom danced with death, Macy and her grandma saved me. Her granny became a surrogate parent to me, staying up late while she knitted and we watched TCM classics together while Macy was droolingly asleep on the dog-hair-covered couch. I'd leave late in the night, lint-brushing myself as I walked through the empty parking lot. Maybe stopped for a too-late slice and garlic dipping sauce at the Pizza Pizza on my way to the seventeenth floor of my decrepit apartment.

There was a gigantic Black dude who lived down the hall who always reeked of weed. I liked the smell though and liked to stand next to him in the elevator. He never said a word to me and we would usually look past each other.

He had to have been three hundred pounds and I was pretty sure he was a pimp since there were different women around all the time. But, then there was a strange white woman in her fifties who always had a smile turned upside down on her face and she was some level of amputee; I couldn't tell because I didn't want to stare.

And down the hall was an OCD nurse who would turn the door handle five times when she left. Once, we left our apartments at the same time and she didn't get to finish her routine because I was standing right there. She joined me in the elevator and when we hit the ground floor, she didn't step out and stayed put. I knew she was going all the way back up so she could properly attend to her doorknob ritual. I didn't begrudge her but I'm pretty sure I called her a freak in my head. What an asshole thing to think.

When Macy and I were a couple, she invited me to stay at her house for Christmas. My mom had passed away and I remember lying in her bed, as Macy would sleep in her grandma's bed when I was over, and I just cried and cried. It was my first Christmas without her and Macy came by my side and asked if I was all right. I replied, 'I will be.'

The whole neighbourhood was strange; it had a tonne of crime as it was close to the Russell projects but there were suburban-looking houses inexplicably tucked in there, with a massive old people demographic as well.

The guy next door to Macy would come over and charge to mow the lawn, shovel the laneway and give rides in his pick-up. He insisted on getting paid though. It was likely a necessary source of income for him as well as dropping off bottles to the LCBO in exchange for a few coins.

Living in that Elmvale apartment was sobering. I had mentioned that murder across the street in the grocery store parking lot and all I remember was waking up and seeing yellow caution tape way down there on a rainy morning. Who knew what to think? Was this type of incident normal around here?

I didn't have internet access at my place and only used the library across the street. There was an odd gentleman who would always book the same computer at the library, with excessively large keys and a blocked screen that you couldn't see unless you stared straight at the screen. Once I spied that he was looking at all sorts of bizarre porn, likely on the 'unfiltered' setting. In the middle of a library.

Then there was the guy who knocked on my door at three a.m. (not sure what I was doing up) but I, stupidly, snuck to the door and peeped a rather stoic-looking gentleman staring right back at me. I was terrified, frozen on the stained tile. I didn't move and waited for him to leave. Could he have been a junkie looking for something? Maybe a dealer used to live here? What the hell was I doing in this goddamn place? I grew up in the damn suburbs of Blackburn Hamlet.

There were immigrants that lived above me. The food they would make would go down the vents and into my kitchen and would create a terrible and inescapable reek. I invested in a strong fan and would place it on top of my stove and would blow back the stink right back at them. It was a minor protest but one I was equipped to make.

I had never lived alone before and had never spent Christmas or New Year alone. Usually, it was with my family but with them gone their separate ways, and not getting invited to Macy's until the following year, I spent the holidays alone. I went to the Metro on Walkley and got a little roast chicken, that always seemed to err on the side of gelatinous goo as opposed to crispy roast. I sat in my apartment, watching the Midnight Mass that the Pope would host while he said something or other in Latin, eating poultry leftovers from earlier in the evening while following it with a boxed banana cream pie. New Year's wasn't much better.

I never really knew the St. Laurent area except for going to the NuDen strip club with my friends when I was in my late teens. We went to strip clubs at an alarming frequency when I was that age. It wasn't even to do anything salacious. We simply drank watered-down beer in pitchers while watching the strippers on 'pervert's row' as it was called. It was at a strip club in Hull where I was so drunk, I kept yelling 'white power' and somehow was not asked to leave. They didn't seem as discerning over the bridge. I couldn't say I ever really enjoyed going to these clubs but it functioned as some sort of Friday ritual, with the occasional Saturdays thrown in. We wouldn't say much and would just park, while we commented on whose breasts were bigger, more petite, pointier, saggier, etc. And the veteran strippers were always good for a laugh because they would throw in parlour tricks like swinging around and around like Olympic gymnasts at the uneven bars. They flew around naked with some serious gusto; they almost spilt my beer right in my face with their missile feet.

When my brother stopped by my apartment (the one and only time he came by), he parked his BMW in the lot. In the elevator, he was standing next to two sketchy guys, who commented on his Argentina soccer hoodie and also his bag which contained a brand-new video camcorder, well before the notion of filming entire movies on your phone. My brother, who resembled a jellyfish squirming on the beach, was hit by this comment: 'That's a nice video camera.' Good grief. The dentist in the Bimmer never returned to lovely Elmvale after that gentle hostility.

Macy had told me that the building had an illegal mosque. I felt I had to have my 'Brown guy' card revoked because I had no idea what that even meant. Apparently, due to space restrictions, several Arabs and Somalis were using one of the tiny apartments as their place of worship. The only problem was that they were attempting to put fifty men into said apartment at one time; it was a serious fire hazard and one that made me feel a bit shaky. One day, I hit the elevator button whose light was broken (shock) so nobody knew if the button had been pressed or not. I gave it another hit and heard the elevator ding. As the doors opened, there stood ten Somali men in white robes, sandals and seriously orange beards. Two thoughts crossed my mind: a) These guys must have been to the illegal mosque since their notion of fire safety, or lack thereof, is consistent with apartments and also evidently elevators, and b) I didn't feel like I belonged here or anywhere else for that matter.

'How many times have we been to CHEO with Daisy?'

'Like for emergencies or just for appointments?'

'Emergencies.'

'A few. A couple of times for croup cough. Fever. Strep throat.'

'Why do kids always seem to get these issues at night. The emergency room is always packed to the goddamn brim. It's the most depressing sight in the world. A helpless child and you're trapped with fifty other people.'

'It's insane.'

'Could you imagine that many people, who are all fucking sick mind you, in one room with no masks on?'

Macy smiled in recognition. It wasn't one of her smiles where she wanted me to shut up; I got plenty of those. This one I could feel she was really mulling over.

'I don't think I'll ever go into an enclosed space without a mask on ever again,' she said.

'Yeah, I don't either. And everybody's like how is my child going to grow up in this? Well, that's what it is, you fucking Karen. Love your child and let them know it's all good instead of handing them a Nintendo Switch for eight hours a day.'

'It is pretty fucked up though.'

'What?'

'Daisy has to wear a mask probably for years.'

'She won't know any different. This will be her reality.'

'Yeah, it's just weird. I'm not sure how I feel about it.'

'I know.'

Macy suddenly gleamed. 'Remember we'd always make fun of all the Asians for wearing masks on regular days? In malls and stuff.'

'Yeah,' I chuckled.

'We were like oh here we go. Some guys down from

Markham and Newmarket wearing their masks again.'

'Apparently Newmarket's gentrified now… just a side note.'

'How did we go to work in the middle of flu season with people hacking all over each other and touching cups and copiers and everything else before all this? How did we not distance ourselves, wear masks and sani up?'

'I have no goddamn idea. And people are like this is going to spawn a generation of germophobes. Our kids will be fucked up. And our immune systems need to be recharged. We can't just not be sick… I'm like what the fuck are all you people on about? Everybody's an epidemiologist suddenly. Every Karen's got some opinion about how our internal biology will be affected by all of this. Just go back to not parenting and shut the fuck up.'

'Do you ever shut the fuck up?'

I was slightly taken aback by this but decided to take it in stride and volley back.

'Not that I'm aware of. It's on my to-do list though.'

'I'm serious. I don't mean joking your way out of my question like some smarmy asshole.'

Apparently, Macy was on to my strategy. Being together for over a decade had not surprisingly unveiled my better tactics.

'Yes, I got you.'

'Got what?'

'I get it. I'm complaining like an asshole and I'm sorry.'

'Do you think I want to hear you piss and moan about everything?'

'Well yes. That's what marriage is, right? We laugh and have a good time but I can vent on you as well, right?'

'This isn't venting. It's non-stop bitching.'

'You wanna keep your voice down? Daisy's down, remember?'

'She's fine. She's out.'

I breathed deeply and really thought about what to say next. Instinct was sometimes a failure in situations like this where Macy could fly into a frenzy of histrionics.

'We... just haven't had any help in a year and a half. Eighteen months with nobody to help with Daisy. Full workdays, working remotely. Full school days where we have to home-school Daisy and walk her through virtual school. And take care of the house. And survive during COVID... and fucking nobody will help us. We only have each other. Just the three of us. Some help this past year and a half would have been good. Just a fucking day here or there. I'm good. I'm just, like, past exhaustion... so I might bitch a bit. Sorry.'

Macy stared straight ahead and didn't immediately react.

'Fine... and yes. I know.'

I considered that a relief more than a victory. I was serious in my sentiment though. We drove by Elmvale to see Macy's old house.

'They widened the laneway.'

'And they got interlocking. Like every other asshole during COVID. We've got all this money from not taking any trips down south so we could sit on a beach and drink all day out of our Yetis or Bubbas or whatever the fuck those tubs full of alcohol are called. So, let's spend our money on something. How about interlocking? Yes, very original. Let's all do that.'

Macy couldn't hide a smile. She gritted her teeth as she gazed ahead, but her attempts made her look like a creepy prison inmate. She let out some grunts of approval. Victory.

CHAPTER TWELVE

Macy stared straight ahead. A windshield wiper blurring her POV a bit. We're so used to layers and layers of matter blocking our eyelines that it's difficult to sometimes simply see something in the way it was intended to be seen. We accept the molested perspective in front of us and accept it without resistance. Almost placating some omniscient irritant by avoiding conflict and routinely allowing this opaque-ing of our preferred widescreen shot.

She was in a bit of a haze. I got trapped in those moments as well and attempting to knock one out of that mini reverie was akin to waking a sleepwalker. She was looking far off into the vista. I wonder what she was thinking about. Her mind was always active and she found it difficult to fall asleep at night because of the need to think about everything, regardless of whether it could be actioned or not. Not easy to action something at one a.m. but she, and many others like her, felt that just thinking about them could at least achieve something.

We drove down Ogilvie Road and slowly passed Gloucester High School, where I had gone from grades nine through thirteen, back when there was something as arbitrary and bizarre as a thirteenth grade. Just based on popular superstition, one would have thought they'd have done away with that frightful grade for its numerical spookiness alone. Not to mention how taxing it is for a teenager to attend a full additional year of high school, like the requisite number wasn't fucking awful enough.

'Mind if I pull in here?'

Macy didn't say anything or even grunt in recognition. She offered a breath that seemed not in line with the previous ones so I interpreted that as approval.

'Thanks, love… I just wanna see what the place looks like. It's been a while… not sure why I wanna see it exactly. I hated it then so not sure if it's gonna be any different now.'

I shut my mouth and crept the car along. There were no cars in the parking lot. Just brown grass and crooked fences and parking paint lines and curbs and windows and decrepit-looking brick and siding and football goal posts and the sign of the school with a green alligator mascot. Not much to 'and' on top of that.

How much I despised going to that school. The place itself wouldn't have made a difference. Macy, in one of her woke moments, would say how every high school in Ottawa was rife with drugs and general criminal activity. Her school, Hillcrest, had drug dog raids. According to her, all the high schools were dripping with sketch and cocaine use was not just recreational but the standard. I was sceptical of this, but it had been a while since I had sauntered down these antiseptic halls with that exclusively teenaged aloof gait.

Ottawa high schools had a high immigrant quotient so at least I felt like I belonged somehow. The yearbook would have Ahmed, Ahmad, Ahmed, Ahmed, and then Anderson to whiten the page a bit. And the 'M' portion was always classic. Mohammed, Mohammad, Mohammed, and about fifteen more until we found more crystallised sugar in the way of Morrison and Moffatt. Brown sugar and then some condensed milk. Vanilla extract with a dash of baking powder.

I was typical in that I had no sense of style, was invisible to girls (and who would blame them), had a giant afro that I thought was acceptable but really had no idea, and had the typical anxiety-ridden social cluelessness that I at least shared with ninety per cent of the student body. Why not for the sake of novelty didn't I step out of that idiotic behaviour and fix myself up? And my afro wasn't even smooth like a Black guy's. I didn't have a comb that I could plant inside the coarse shrubbery the way some Black dudes did at the school. I instead had a semi-soft, semi-coarse, sort of wavy, mostly messy and full shit show perched on top of my head. It had no sense of cohesion. Just dirty looking and unkempt. There didn't seem to be any sense of order and most people caught on that I didn't like to brush my hair in the morning. I caught this exchange once between a couple of Chads referring to my fro:

'Bad hair day I guess.'

'I know!'

And somehow, it didn't change my ways. I was too dumb and aloof to even engage with this commentary. I didn't have the balls to confront them. I was too unaware for it to get me down; how much further down could I go? And I wasn't proactive enough to listen to this sage advice and action something to enhance my appearance a bit. The best I looked in high school was when I shaved my head a few times. It turned me from a grimy scrub into a semi-decent-looking cat. But the cretin that I am, I didn't pick up on the positive social signals I was receiving so I reverted back to the 'poet look'; in other words, homeless and lonely.

I looked out at the front of the school. There used to be smokers teeming from spot to spot in those days. The school board made it clear that all smokers needed to situate themselves at the front of the school, to be away from all the students who didn't want to be around second-hand smoke. But the drawback to this was that all the people driving by could see over a hundred kids, from thirteen to fifteen years old usually, smoking in front of the logo of the school mascot. Thirteen-year-old kids smoking. What in the world was going on? Every time a kid would arrive late to class reeking of smoke, it made me shudder. Being a sheltered kid at least had an upside. I wonder what it's like now. Do kids smoke like that now? Do they still do it in front of the school?

Back then, it made me feel sick because of the nicotine stench. Whether it was regular cigarettes or the native contraband ones, all of them made me feel nauseated. Now, it makes me sick for different reasons. How will Daisy react when somebody asks if she wants to smoke? Will she fall for it? Succumb? Will she get belligerent and tell them to fuck off? Shrug them off politely and say it's not her thing? Sneer at them and make them feel inferior? Confidently say 'no thanks' without a whisper of pretention. God, I wish it's the last one.

How can Daisy stay who she is in these trenches? Other kids are just proxies of their shitty parents. The asshole financial planner or investment portfolio manager selling off bespoke tranche opportunities to unsuspecting novices. The real estate managers. Lawyers. Or the best one – consultants. Those fluff pricks who rob people blind with their unspeakable lack of talent or knowledge in anything and everything. There will be kids who will be hanging around Daisy who have these schmucks as parents. Parents at it again – the true pandemic.

I peered inside the windows as I crawled the car metre by metre. I couldn't see inside either because of the grime (likely), 1970s windows lacking in any sort of clarity (quite likely), or they were tinted (highly unlikely).

The lobby was the wide hallway on the main floor of

Gloucester High. The place where every clique congregated to feel welcomed by others and feel apart from all others. It was social distancing before a virus made it official. The ceiling of the lobby was covered with hand-painted canvases reflecting personal expression and cultural identity. The school was big on that. I once, in a rush of wanting to be a part of something, joined an International Cultures United meeting. Since I was Brown, I felt I had a passport in. I went for one meeting and after hearing an incoherent opening monologue by the Haitian teacher leading the group, and then a subsequent and equally incoherent and rambling speech by his underling, an Iraqi Canadian girl in a hijab sporting a pretty mean look, I decided that one meeting was enough. I had better shit to do anyway. Like get home and masturbate to the *Sports Illustrated* swimsuit issue, back when that was actually a thing. The magazine, not the masturbation. The former has had its epitaph finalised, while the latter will proceed until 'the last syllable of recorded time.'

I had one teacher who was so surly, but he was so damn brilliant, his demeanour became entertaining. He had printed copies of his favourite poetry on the walls of his English class residing in a portable. Schools had a way of eschewing actual building renovations by creating portables that you could have classes in; essentially, makeshift caravans that were freezing cold in the winter and scorching hell in the near-summer, and always baffling to set foot in, like you were joining a band of travelling carnies.

This teacher would challenge the class and declare, 'When you write an essay, *say* something.' It doesn't seem like much to hear that now but to the green ears of an idealistic kid, this kind of thing was super inspiring. To have a teacher demand that you be creative and express yourself regardless of how moronic it might sound. One of my proudest moments at Gloucester was when he read my essay on how Hamlet was in fact a dark comedy to the entire class. Getting that uplift from a real teacher who knew what he was talking about was so reassuring. It didn't draw me out of my cocoon of crippling shyness, but it was a millimetre in the right direction. I wonder if that teacher is still alive.

I came back to Gloucester years before because I needed a copy of my high school diploma for some records for when I was applying to Algonquin College. I suddenly realised how much things had changed over time. The fear and the justifiable caution. I couldn't just roam the halls, with sporadic nods of recognition and nostalgia, and think it'd be okay. I had to clear my presence at the school with the school admins at front desk, sign in and state my reason for being there. I was nineteen and finished my first year at Ottawa U when the Columbine massacre happened. The notion of school shooters was so alien that it just didn't figure into the equation. We knew most of the student population hated school, hated themselves and hated their antagonists so much they fantasised about what the Columbine shooters had done. But the idea of actually doing that was so abhorrent and senseless, it did not compute. High schoolers were too cut off from reality to let their extreme emotions actually allow them to action anything. It was easier to cry or play video games or read or be nihilistic.

The admins gave me the diploma and charged me $30 for their troubles with a GHS invoice with a gator on it; they were consistent I gave them that. Devoid of cash, I asked if there was an ATM at the school, perhaps in the lobby. They sneered with a mixture of snobbery and quizzical looks. I sneered at their sneer. The lobby had several vending machines so it didn't seem out of the realm of possibility that there would also be an ATM in order to allow these sickly pimpled teens to eat their feelings with a measure of pragmatism.

I stopped the car for a second and Macy just stared out the window, deep in reflection, but of what I did not know. Daisy napped and I wished I was napping. Each day had become a siege of trying to find five minutes to nap. If I could take a month off like government workers, I would spend the first two days in bed, not getting up at all. Only to drop Daisy off at school and pick her up. The rest would be spent in bed, charging the battery up my own ass like we charge the iPad over and over. I wish I worked at Portage or one of those other government buildings. I did my co-op placements at Health Canada and Public Service Commission and to say that most of these workers were worthless would be a vast understatement. Collecting cheques for what I cannot say. Lazy, inept and badge-wearing.

A surge hit me. I remembered my last year at Gloucester High. A kid was nearly killed. My buddies and I were in the cafeteria and were laughing heartily while playing 'Would You Rather?' Apparently, my friends would rather drink a glass of diarrhoea over eating a bowlful of shit (in log form). The rationale for this went on for a few minutes and it was in these puerile moments that I forgot how much I hated the school and loved having close friends to laugh with.

The back of the cafeteria was lined with windows and in the far-off distance, you could see the football field and we saw some sort of commotion. It wasn't anything that we considered to be important. Just a scuffle.

Later, a hijab girl said to a classmate, 'I heard there was a really bad fight.'

I interjected with, 'Nothing happened. It was just a lot of show.' I actually had no idea but felt the need to offer my unsolicited opinion.

My schoolmate scrunched up his face and said, 'Yeah it did. Some kid got the shit kicked out of him.'

I was silent. The hijab girl said, 'So sad when it's our last year here and so close to summer.'

I didn't understand how either of those two points were relevant to anything. It's sad because it affects our final year? We wished for our grade thirteen year to be unsullied, I suppose? What if it had happened the following year? Would that have made it less horrific? And so close to summer? Who gives a shit when it happened? Getting beat down doesn't get better or worse based on seasonal variation.

The kid was a Somali. Apparently, he had said something derogatory about some Chad's girlfriend and some random Brock who was a friend of the aforementioned white guy came at the Black kid like a white knight. There was blood. There were black eyes. A jaw needed to be wired shut. There were broken ribs. There was an ambulance. And it all happened to the Somali kid.

There was so much rage in the subsequent week. The PA system had an announcement talking about the malicious attack and how that student was to be expelled and potentially charged. The cafeteria chats were no longer about silly things but about something real for a change. A significant and possibly racially motivated assault. As a Brown guy, I felt like I spoke for the minorities since there were so many Middle Easterns at our school.

The school staged an awkward and tension-filled assembly in which some Muslim scholars came in to engage the students in a discourse about their religion and the need for tolerance. This was one year before Columbine but I felt I had drunk my first glass of that potion no kid ever wants to imbibe. That sting of fruity red wine. It felt sweet to be an adult and understand a new paradigm that didn't solely consist of myself. But the initiation into the world of the real. It was all too much. The sediment was gravelly and harsh. I wasn't sure I wanted to go, but the horse and carriage had already pulled away and I was in that stagecoach.

'I think I'm done, Macy.

'Are you good?'

'Me, yeah I'm good.'

'Did you get what you came for?'

'Um, I'm not sure what I was even looking for. Just wanted to see this place for some reason.'

'Can we go?'

'Yes, we can. I fucking hate this place. I wish it would burn to the ground so they could build another Walmart. That's how much I hate this place.'

'They should just burn all the schools down and make them all virtual.'

I wasn't sure if she was kidding or not, but I didn't respond.

I had just turned seventeen years old when our World Religions class in grade twelve took us on a field trip. The 'field trip' concept is rather absurdist. The notion of being herded into a loudly painted yellow school bus, in the middle of the day when you are expected to be in class learning; driving away from school in rather a melancholy manner in the full knowledge that you'll be coming back later in the day; feeling like you're being truant when you're really just hanging out with your asshole classmates and your asshole teacher; observing the same school bus seat hierarchy in which the pricks sit at the back and the losers sit at the front, and the invisibles sit right in the meaty middle; the teacher urging everyone to bring a lunch but nobody listening because eating a 'brought' lunch on a field trip would make you look like a loser; and, most glaringly of all, spending time with your teacher outside of the school perimeter, almost making it seem as if you're spending time with him when all you'd like to do is perform seppuku to end the field trip.

We first went to a Catholic church downtown, I think around Elgin Street, in which we had to take our hats off and act solemnly in front of a stained-glass window. And there were people there, like, praying and observing.

After grabbing a vanilla cone with my Brown buddy (he was devoutly Muslim and… I needed somebody to hang out with, so I didn't have to eat lunch out of my grocery store plastic bag alone). He had his cone and we got back on the bus, on our way to a synagogue. This time, we had to wear our hats, and if you didn't have one, you got some dandruffy cloth to place on your head instead. The Rabbi was pretty funny. He was that typical vision of a Rabbi that I had always had: a sardonic short old guy with square fingernails, an oversized suit and a Bronx drawl. Strange that he sounded like a New Yorker even in downtown Ottawa. Do all the Rabbis go to some sort of DIY Talmud learning facility in New York and then disperse to wherever they're needed?

After that fun little jaunt, we went to a mosque, that was more African vibe than Arab. The guy, I think he was Somali, went through the cleansing ritual in a latrine-like facility. He proceeded to show us how to wash our hands, eyes, ears, feet (even between the toes), and then the nose, and then ending with a symphonic flourish as he horked a gob of snot down the drain hole. The experience was thoroughly delightful. I'm sure he said some stuff referencing the Quran but all I remember was the hork trying to nudge itself down the drain but having too much density to do so. Imagine if we had this guy's ritualistic hygiene tutorials, maybe COVID never would have happened.

And we rounded the trip off with an excursion to the Sikh temple on Gurdwara Road, close to where we live now in Riverside South. It was entertaining as they busted out some cool string instruments and played some Indian vibey music for us. They even gave us barbecue-flavoured chips and Cokes. One of the students said, 'Their generosity is astounding.' That was a weird thing to say I thought. What, you thought they'd be selfish pricks? Or that's how you'd expect Indians or Pakistanis to be? Or wherever the fuck they were from. The main Sikh guy kept saying 'guru or teacher', and then this gormless student pipes up, 'What's a guru?' Well, in class we had learnt that gurus were teachers like fifty times, and this raghead in front of us just fucking said 'guru *or* teacher.' Jesus... I mean, Vishnu. And as the stereotype would have it, the place smelled like curry. And even worse, the rags we had to put on our heads, smelled like curry as well. So, we sauntered back into our classrooms near the end of the day with 'curry head,' eliciting some strange looks from the douchebags in Von Dutch hats.

The next morning, in World Religions class, we reminisced about our journey into the religious netherworld of Ottawa. Monotonous organ music and Stars of David. No-name brand potato chips and used latrines. We somehow started talking about circumcision. One kid said, 'If you're not circumcised, it means your mother didn't love you.'

CHAPTER THIRTEEN

The Nissan Rogue ambled on like a fat ant. Pitch black exterior with an equally charcoally upholstery situation inside. Boiling in the summer and frostbitten in windchill season. So dusty, one could barely read the radio station. Built-in CD player still in place; probably one of the last in existence. Pounding Bose speakers to let the bass pulsate off the semi-tinted windows. Gravel under foot; remnants from the previous winter's salt rock from common pavements now residing on the floor mats. Grease mark on the head rest from the driver's bald head; crown shining proudly.

SUVs are always something I despised but not as much as mini-vans. It felt like a cliché to hate mini-vans but they really were vile, weren't they? Everything that reeked of Karens lived in the membrane of a mini-van. What was it about them? The tacky sliding doors or the hockey equipment reek in the trunk. Or the animal cracker crumbs everywhere. The stench of beauty bar perfume on sale with stale shawarma with overdone whipped garlic.

'Did you play here?'

'At Hornet's Nest?'

'Yeah.'

'Nope never played there. I didn't actually start playing soccer until I was twenty-two.'

'Seriously?'

'Yeah. I only know indoor though. Futsal. I like the five-on-five game. It's like quick touch, quick touch. The outdoor game. I don't even know how to play it. I'd be lost out there. I'm used to tight spaces and quick touches.'

I could sense Macy wavering. Did I offer too much information about soccer? I didn't presume that just because she was a girl, she wouldn't give a shit about sports. But maybe I should have presumed that very thing since ninety-nine per cent of the girls I'd known in my life hated sports and didn't know shit about them. Was it perhaps conceivable that the stereotype was true about women being disinterested in sports? If I were to take a random sample of women from different demographics, what are the odds that most of them would have an even basic handle on sports history, sports strategy, names, dates, etc.? Why does this kind of thing anger people? Why wasn't it okay to say most women hate sports and a very small minority feels the opposite? Was I an asshole for pointing this out? I didn't point it out though. I just thought it. Did that still make me an asshole?

'Sorry for rambling on there about indoor soccer.'

'You weren't rambling,' Macy said with a warm smile.

'I miss playing so much. I didn't think I'd miss it this much.'

'You miss the boys.'

'Yeah, I do but just playing, you know? The competition. Grinding each game. Sweating. Trash talking the other team.'

'I don't see it coming back for a while.'

'What if the numbers don't go up? We're like three quarters vaccinated in Ottawa. A lot are fully vaccinated.'

'I know.'

'So, maybe we outrun this wave.'

'Maybe.'

'What, you don't think so?'

'I don't know.'

'Why don't you think so? The modelling shows it. The spike was supposed to happen, but it didn't take and now the same will probably happen with this wave.'

'Are you trying to convince me or yourself?'

'It's just science and mathematics.'

'Yeah. And it's just you guys playing in schools after hours.'

'So?'

'You really think the school board is going to be okay with having the futsal league doing what they usually do? Playing in schools all over the city every Wednesday and Thursday night? Letting a bunch of outsiders into the building when they're trying to keep all the cohorts tight and ordered? Are you crazy? There's no way you guys have a season this year. Would you want a bunch of random guys coming in and out of the school when you can't deep clean it?'

I sat there in silence for what felt like minutes, but I couldn't keep my oversized mouth closed for more than a few seconds.

'Guess you're right. Sorry I wanted to fucking fantasise that I'd get to play again.'

'I know you want to play. But don't be such a big bitch.'

Macy's soliloquy on my soccer season ending before it began didn't shut me up but her last remark did. I breathed; perhaps deeper than I needed to.

'What?' Macy interjected.

'What?'

'What was that? Are you pissed?'

'I just breathed.'

'Yeah, I know that breathing. And your mouth is slightly open and you're looking far into the distance. You're pissed at me.'

'So, first you're an amateur epidemiologist and now you're

fucking Jung. Nice.'

'Why not just say Freud? Is that too obvious for you and you have to be different, so you say Jung? Even though you don't know fuck-all about either of them?'

This was the verbal equivalent of a UFC fighter drop-kicking some hapless schmuck and coaxing him into a delicate slumber. That fateful moment when you see a guy's instep land on his opponent's jaw, turning his face into strawberry jelly, and his legs into fusilli. Macy had that way of sizing me up and making me look like such an asshole. Not just a boorish asshole but a transparent one too. It wasn't exactly enjoyable getting picked apart like that. If I ever did that to her, I'd be accused of being a mentally abusive gas lighter. But, if people had seen the way Macy eviscerated me, they'd applaud her and call her spunky and assertive. Strange how that pendulum swung. Weren't women always called bitches for that kind of thing? Now, in the Me Too era, they can do no wrong. Probably a good thing though. We could use more women world leaders. Maybe they can fix this cesspool. Bring back some love and save the planet for girls like Daisy.

Macy looked past Hornet's Nest as we passed it. It was one of the more known soccer fields in Ottawa. Those large domes that are freakishly cold in the winter, so you're always nuzzled by the heaters.

'It's like a Karen pandemic down there,' Macy said. I chuckled. She continued. 'They've probably got their LV bags as well with their high maintenance friends…'

We drove on and let the Karens live their lives, complaining to the managers about their Tim Horton's coffee. The dark roast just isn't good enough. Like everything else on the damn menu. Who could blame them for making a fuss? The bagels taste like erasers and there's enough bland cream cheese on those concoctions to feed a small village. The bacon, which is not even actual bacon, tastes like wood chips. And everything generally tastes like decay. I knew it was blasphemy to say anything against the gospel of Tim Horton's but I felt it absurd to extol the virtues of something that tasted so noxious. Weren't there things that were better to be proud of? Parliament Hill? National Gallery with that giant spider outside with the egg sac hanging off it? Museum of Civilisation? Bluesfest? All the shawarma restaurants (strangely, hardly any of them are any good; take it from a Brown guy)? All those wonderful icons but Tim Horton's somehow transcends the norm and ascends to impermeability. Inexplicable.

'I can't believe you grew up around here,' Macy interjected into my thoughts again.

'What's the big deal? It's the same shit as anywhere else.'

'Welcome to Blackburn Hamlet. God, it's so suburby.'

'Yeah, it is. Not a fan of that but I grew up here. Didn't really have a say in the matter.'

I lived here with my family for seventeen years. In today's world of house-hopping, flipping, and over-usage of obnoxious real estate terms like 'reno' and 'gutting', it seems like a miracle to be in a house for longer than three years.

Whenever you talk to people, space always seems to be an issue. I was never sure why people needed that much space and what they intended to do with it. Were they attempting to cultivate a cornfield indoors? Or did they hate their kids and spouses to such a spectacular degree that custom designing a home that inserted a football field-sized space between them would be the only way they could function?

When we take Daisy to the park or the play structure, Macy and I are the only ones not on our phones and not talking about house décor. We do this strange thing called watching our child and smiling and cheering her on and giving a shit about what she's doing with pride. And when we can see her out of the corner of our eyes, we do this truly bizarre thing called talking to each other.

It's mystifying how rarely we see couples actually talking to each other. Have couples ever spoken to each other or is it a generational thing? Macy and I always felt like we were looked at like we were Martians because we weren't incessantly on our phones, and we were actually talking and laughing with each other. The paranoid part of people's brains probably falsely intuited that we were talking about them.

But the Blackburn Hamlet neighbourhood was the standard idyllic look for a kid. Convenience stores where you could bike down with your friends to have giant freezies while sitting on the curb. Playing baseball in the local diamonds. Playing basketball on the local courts. Renting videos from the mom-and-pop shops down the street like Videoflicks. Playing video games in cool basements on hot days. It was utterly normal with no semblance of the sinister until we grew up and started seeing things with more clarity.

I remember shooting hoops with my buddies. In the Emily Carr Middle School courts where there were night-time lights. Dusty courts were always, for some reason, covered in sand. These Brown guys came down to play us once. It was a weird moment for me since I was a fellow Brown guy but not a stereotypical one. I had the fob hair but I had lost that a bit when I shaved my head, so my entire look changed in one sword thrust.

These guys were all wearing wife-beaters and smelled like fried onions and kabobs. I was pathologically afraid of leaving the house smelling of Iranian food scents like dried fenugreek but these guys were completely devoid of that kind of self-consciousness.

The courts would typically have the smell of skunk weed floating around. When in Orient Park, the sketchy underbelly of Blackburn, the courts were usually rife with weirdos and shady characters. I was so green, I once asked, on behalf of my friends and me, if these guys shooting around wanted to have a game. The head guy, a Black guy with a seemingly vacant look about him, shot me a steely glare and said, 'I'm in my slippers.' I didn't press the issue and went back to my friends with no challengers, completely feeling emasculated and slightly threatened.

Emily Carr Middle School was a place in which I saw and did things I wished I hadn't. I was the pathetic kid who was sometimes picked on but didn't have the balls to stand up for anyone else. One day, a girl of, I think, Eastern European descent, was sitting in her chair and everybody was sticking gum to the back of her shirt. This went way beyond the puerile 'Kick me' signs that kids from the 1950s would use. This was downright cruel. Several of us would chew our gum and smack the residue onto her back and say, 'How ya doin'?' in order to mask the gum-sticking and make it look like a pat on the back; a gesture of salutation. I was the least brutal of the bunch as my gum was pretty dry but the others used just recently-chewed pink bubble gum which stained her shirt. I was still a terrible culprit though. The next day, she said to me directly, 'Thanks for sticking that gum on my back. My parents couldn't get the stains out.' God, what a worthless piece of garbage I was. How could I do such a thing? Who was that kid?

There was a kid I always hung out with after school. In eighth grade, I had gained a little traction in terms of actually having a reputation. I was known, along with my friend, as being the guy in class who felt superior and made cutting remarks about everyone's stupidity, ignorance and lack of creativity. Essentially, we were hateful morons. We'd chuck a Nerf football around after everybody had gone home and then pop over to the local doughnut shop to get a maple dip and a Coke. When we were sitting, we saw a girl from our school with a stroller. She was fourteen. This was too much for me to compute at that age. When my buddy told me she was a mom, my thirteen-year-old brain didn't know how to take it. How could you have just gotten out of middle school and be a fucking parent?

Right down the street was Orient Park and across the street was where the old Reddi Chef used to be where we'd get hot wedge fries on those classic windchill days. And the old Winks was where I'd pop in and steal grape-flavoured Bubble King gum.

On one of those late afterschool afternoons, when my friend and I were hanging out, and making our way up the steep hill home, there were two girls walking up the same hill ahead of us; one red-headed and thin, while the other was brunette and overweight. We started throwing snowballs at the fatter one and laughed, while yelling, 'Don't worry!' to the redhead. 'We won't throw them at you! You're too thin!' Eventually, we pegged the fat one so many times in the back that she stopped where she stood and cried to the heavens. The redhead looked at us and mournfully said, 'Guys. Come on.'

'God, I fucking loathe this neighbourhood.'

'Make your way down Innes and get out of here.'

'Going.'

'What's the big deal?'

'I just hate this place. Hate who I was back then and hate that I could never be that guy who could stand up and be worth something.'

'God, why do you always get so nostalgic?'

'I'm not being nostalgic. I'm just being reflective. There's a difference. I have no nostalgia for this place. Those are years I'd rather forget and a person I'd rather kill off, but he's stuck in my head.'

'God, you're such a drama queen.'

'You never think about that stuff. You had a good upbringing. Was everything at Vincent Massey and Hillcrest normal?'

'Basically. I had fun. It was like normal. I don't get it when people said it was like hell for them. I don't really think about it. I wasn't popular or anything. It was just, like, whatever.'

'Did you have bullying or shit like that at your schools?'

'Only a bit but not much.'

'Bullshit.'

'We really didn't. Or at least I didn't see it. Our principal did get punched in the face once though.'

I reluctantly blurted out a laugh.

'And that guy was the vice principal at Gloucester when I was there.'

'That's right, you told me,' she smirked. 'We had a connection even back then.'

Macy always knew what corny shit would make me smile.

'Most of the kids at Vincent Massey and Hillcrest were Somali immigrants or people from countries that got torn up. Everybody kind of felt like outsiders. There weren't that many "popular" kids,' she continued.

'Yeah.'

'It was fun though. But because of dance practices, I didn't get to go to school dances on Fridays. That kind of sucked. That would've been fun.'

'Yeah. I don't think I even went to one. They were all in the lobby.'

Macy smiled, 'Oh yeah. That place.'

'And we were always like, 'Guy, why you wanna go to the school dance? It's lame, guy. Guy, why you going, guy?''

'Oh God, you were one of those losers? Who said "guy" all the time? All the Lebs said that.'

'Not just the Lebs. All Brown guys. That was ours.'

'God, it was so fucking stupid.'

'Yeah, I agree. But whatever. I just really wanna get the fuck out of this neighbourhood.'

'Drive on, Brown boy.'

On our way out of Blackburn, we passed Tauvette Park. My friends and I frequented this baseball diamond many a time. We'd never have enough guys to have a real game, so we invented games like groundball drills and homerun derbies, but those days were boss. The clink of the aluminium bat against the many boxes of baseballs we went through. The dug-in area where we'd get our stance ready in the batter's box. The humid-smelling green, green grass. The black piping across the top of the outfield fence so you could jump up and rob potential dingers. The meditative feel of a ball popped way up in the sky until it resembled a gnat hanging under the clouds for a fleeting moment until making its way down. Breathing calmly as it torpedoed down and nestled itself in your worn-in glove. If it weren't for memories of baseball in that diamond, I'd probably wanna burn that entire fucking neighbourhood to the ground.

CHAPTER FOURTEEN

We sped down Highway 417 at 120 km/hr. I hardly ever went higher than that. I still found that cars were tailgating or trying to bully me out of the way. I didn't even hang out in the passing lane instead parking myself comfortably in the no-nonsense lane, and still found I was seeing the rusty grill of a pick-up behind me. It's not in the DNA of a pick-up truck driver to be chemically balanced. When placed in the cabin of that vehicle, something inexplicable happens to the brain of the driver. All semblance of rationality and social courtesy is aborted in favour of extreme hostility and belligerence. There must be a gas that the auto companies emit into the cabin of a pick-up once the ignition is struck, turning otherwise normal drivers into sociopaths.

I saw a car fly by me on the right side and another on the left side and one behind me trying to box me in, and in a brief in-between moment, death whispered in my ear.

'What's going on?' I said, but I wasn't sure at that moment if I had said it aloud.

'Just checking on you.'

'Don't you have better places to see than Ottawa?'

'I'm stuck here for all of eternity like you.'

'Well, there are worse places than this.'

'I hate this place.'

'I only hate this place sometimes. Most days, it's pretty cool.'

'The city shuts down at nine p.m. There's no nightlife.'

'Who gives a shit? I don't give a fuck about nightlife.'

'There's no culture here.'

'Sure there is. It's just more content than other places. This place is not about intensity. It's mellow and sleepy and I don't mind that.'

'You only have one life. Don't you want to explore the world?'

'I have a family. I can't just pick up and go to Peru to eat that hallucinogenic shit that makes you vomit and supposedly have a spiritual experience. I like it here with them.'

'You're meant to be creative and be an artist and take risks.'

'I don't want to take risks. I love my family. My two girls. They are all.'

'Stop talking stupid.'

'I'm not.'

'Ottawa is a worthless shithole, and you should leave it. You should be in New York. Boston. Rome. Paris.'

'Why does everybody say the same cities? Why don't people say Kabul for once? Or Kashmir?'

'Is that supposed to be funny?'

'Not for the people that live there it's not.'

'I'm being serious.'

'So am I. I like Ottawa. I've only just realised that in the last decade of my life.'

'Idiot.'

'I like all the sentimental shit I hated when I was a kid. I like seeing the Parliament Building on Canada Day. And seeing the beautiful and also awkward sculptures at Winterlude. And lying on the beach at Mooney's Bay and wondering if it's okay to go near that filthy E. coli water. And driving along the Rideau Canal on Colonel By criticizing all the modern custom builds on Echo

Drive, while seeing the sun shimmer off the ripples of the water. I like the Greenbelt. I like fresh loaves from Art-Is-In Bakery and big fat burgers from The Works. I like all the stupid mini-malls. I like walking through Chapters, even when it says Indigo outside. I like pub breakfasts at places like The Highlander, although I'm not sure it exists any more. I like biking through Manotick wondering why people need such self-indulgent homes, and why they went to so much trouble hanging Trudeau hate signs on their manicured lawns. I like lox and bagels at Kettleman's, and brunch at The Belmont. I like walking through the Gay Village on Bank Street and seeing if I can spot a drag queen. I like thinking that someday, I'll visit The Lookout so we can see some real drag queens.'

'Okay enough.'

'I like it here, Mom.'

'There's a real drag queen club here?'

'Yeah, I think Macy had part of her bachelorette party there.'

'I always wanted to go to a drag club.'

'I know you did. I wish we could've had a chance to go.'

'Before that termite ate my insides.'

CHAPTER FIFTEEN

Darius was slender. About six feet tall, just barely, and a bald head, always with a touch of stubble. Brown skin but not super brown. Hair that was routinely man-scaped and a fairly angular look. He wished he could grow a slight beard, but the scruff tickled his neck too much and he couldn't get past that irritating stage to get to the good part where he could sport a proper hipster beard. He used to have an afro in high school but not as put together as a Black guy's fro. It was more of a scraggly Middle Eastern mess of black hair, uncombed and uncaring. The glasses were thick-rimmed and hipster, while the jeans were skinny-fit and hipster, and everything seemed to exude hipster. He liked to switch up his look from business casual to preppy to hipster to street and he felt he was lucky enough to be able to pull off each look with ease.

Macy was a dancer. She grew up dancing, performing in ballet to jazz to lyrical. She had sky blue eyes that smiled but could also burn with ferocious rage. Making her laugh was something Darius could do. Take the laughter out and what's left is a black hole. A relationship without humour is a business meeting in the Twin Towers. She had the slightest freckles on her nose; enough to be charming but not so much to resemble an infestation. She could look good in practically anything. She looked particularly disarming in a tight-fit leather jacket she purchased when they vacationed in Florence when they were both students. Whether her hair was up in a messy bob, dangling pony, sweep-across bangs, shaggy mane or slick-straightened, she was gorgeous. And her pinky toenail was adorable in the way it was almost sunken-in, like a turtle hiding under its shell. She was confident in high school, confident in university and confident at work. There was no change in her; she was a perfect being right from the jump. Darius saw her when they worked part-time jobs and was immediately in a state of rapture.

Daisy was quirky. She was hard-headed like her mom and dad, but aware of everything and observant beyond her years. She was always smiling and dancing and playing. The words, 'hate', 'bored', 'terrible', 'disgusting', or any other shitty negative word for that matter, never came out of her mouth. She was an entirely positive kid with an ideal balance between being solitary and gregarious. The oft-quoted cliché that 'only children' are weird didn't apply to her. She loved being alone, loved being with her parents and loved being with other kids. Whatever was on the menu for the day was okay with her. She inherited her mum's expressive eyes, however trading in the ocean for espresso. She ran like Usain and ate like Kobayashi. Her cup was never full; voracious appetite for the world and all its wonders and irregularities. Her hair down was lovely; hair in a pony was adorable, hair in a braid made Darius swoon, although he promised to do it in his head and not in front of her to spare her the embarrassment. She loved fishy crackers and yoghurt drinks; fluffy rice and kabob from I Cook Persian Cuisine in Little Lebanon. Darius didn't mention that it was an Iranian restaurant in an Arab neighbourhood and just rolled with the Brown theme. She loved music and was curious as to why none of the other kids knew anything about it. Didn't their parents play music in the house she always wondered?

Lansdowne's Pavilion was housing the Van Gogh exhibit

that projected images onto the walls for an intensive and immersive experience. The lineup outside was long but everyone had their tickets on their phones, purchased in advance. There was no such thing as a ticket line any more in the age of COVID; just ticketholders with staggered entry.

A mom and her eleven-year-old daughter were taking pictures of their, likely freshly painted toenails, and more than likely posting to Instagram. A family of five were standing with frowns on their faces. Did they feel like they were fulfilling some required duty to see the Van Gogh exhibit while it was in town?

A twenty-something guy in a Jays hat was standing with his mom and sang the first verse of an immediately recognisable Canadian song and got chastised by his mom for 'embarrassing' her. To ease his discomfort, Darius sang the next line, and the guy's face lit up and blurted out joyfully, 'Hey?' They both shared a moment of feeling like free spirits in a lineup chock full of milk duds.

There were passersby attending the farmer's market right next to the Pavilion. Plenty of wiener dogs to appease the tiny dog lovers and then gargantuan Newfoundlanders traipsing about, bigger than some of the kids there. The Glebe-ites slumming it in the corporate part of the neighbourhood, buying fresh goat cheese and meats. Hand-crafted soaps and kimchi. Falafel wraps made fresh by some Syrians who loved tossing the dough around. Micro-greens and assorted flavours of weird ice cream. Horseradish ice cream? Cuban black bean and cream of parsnip soups. Ethiopian samosas and Argentinian empanadas. This was the Glebe all right.

Everyone had one hour in the Pavilion to see the exhibit. Some patrons stood and revolved around to take it all in. Some stood in the middle while a rare few stood directly in the corners for an iris-out vantage point. Some sat down with their hands behind them propping up their bodies, while others sat and leaned forward. Some sat cross-legged in the Buddha pose while others were on their phones. Some chatted and some were quiet. Some were transfixed while most were baffled and seemingly unimpressed. Most posted photos to social media ensuring that their network knew that they were there and were having a good time.

Daisy looked around her, fascinated for the first half and patience wavering for the second. Macy, who adored Van Gogh, drank and drank in the colour. Darius felt moments of that elusive transcendence.

'Do you think Van Gogh was an angel?' Darius said.

'Maybe.'

'I know you think I'm all down on stuff like that but seriously. What if he was an angel? He was here for a while and saw so much magnificent beauty all around him. Other people just saw things but he saw an explosion everywhere he looked… do you think he was put on the earth for a reason?'

'You know I believe those things.'

'I wonder more about that stuff.'

'I always said so.'

'No, I don't mean being sure of it. I don't like that. I just like being open to it. You're saying you're sure and that's not cool.'

'Well… we disagree.'

They were silent for a few beats as Darius pulled up to a red light, and Daisy's snoring was audible now.

'There were a lot of people on their phones in there.'

'Oh God, don't start.'

'I'm not.'

'Yeah, you are. You're about to.'

'I'm just interested in how people consume things.'

'And how they do it wrong and only you do it right.'

'I didn't say that.'

'You were about to.'

'I'm more open to people using their phones and taking pics and videos and posting stuff. I'm more okay with that stuff than I was like ten years ago.'

Macy quietly bristled.

'You don't believe me?'

'Hmmm.'

'What does that mean?'

'It just seems like you think you're superior because you don't use your phone and other people do. What's wrong with people documenting the places they go and things they do?'

'Nothing. I'm more okay with it than I was before.'

'Doesn't always sound like it. When I pull out my phone to take a pic of a nice-looking breakfast or dinner, you roll your eyes.'

'Wrong. I used to do that. I don't any more. I don't mind it any more.'

'I can see you fighting it.'

'But I don't do it.'

'Then why did you bring up the thing about lots of people being on their phones in the Van Gogh thing?'

'I was just asking because I noticed it. It was just an observation.'

'No, it pissed you off.'

'Wrong. I was just curious. Macy, you don't need to keep telling me how I feel about stuff. I'm not that scruffy dick who used to get pissed off about that stuff.'

'Fine I guess.'

'Why shouldn't people be able to take a pic of a beautiful meal or the places they go? I think people who sneer at that are just assholes who are just enemies of fun. I used to think it was weird to do that but it's fun. There was that critic who said once that if I ask somebody why they did something, and the answer is "fun" then that's a totally acceptable answer and there's nothing more to talk about.'

Macy was quiet. Darius knew she didn't believe him, but he was telling the truth. Since he had known Macy, he had not only changed his context, but he had changed himself. For the better. His upbringing had been shrouded in negativity and who wants to be around toxic assholes all the time. What on earth can be gained?

'So much anguish in that little Dutch man. So much pain and torment, and so much genius.'

'I love him too.'

The light was still red. Darius thought maybe if I creep the car forward, it will activate the thing in the ground at the stop line and the light would change. Was that really a thing? Was there some sort of device in the ground that detected vehicle movement to change the light? Was that an urban myth he had believed all these years?

CHAPTER SIXTEEN

Canadian Tire Centre was Ottawa's arena. TD Place had the Lansdowne area covered in terms of a more 'stadium' experience, but the city only had one legitimate arena and that was the Canadian Tire Centre in Kanata.

TD Place had only been up and running for a few years, when the Lansdowne project came to full fruition, enraging the locals who wanted to uphold the purity of that neighbourhood. And by purity, I mean keeping the Glebe as closeted, insulated and elitist as humanly possible. Only dog-owning, farm-to-table-loving residents were allowed. Self-indulgent bluster was a prerequisite for owning a home in the Glebe. If the plumbing was from the Victorian era, you knew you were standing in a Glebe home.

However, those silly little Glebe-ites did have a point in the end when the Lansdowne area morphed into a next-level monstrosity, slowly eliminating the beloved antique mom-and-pop shops in favour of an antiseptic sheen, designed to bring out families and those in need of a Tinder hook-up alike.

TD Place was where ageing rock and roll bands played and of course modern country stars. Ottawa wasn't a place that existed unto itself; it was a place people from other places migrated to. Ask an Ottawa resident if they were born here and probably eight times out of ten, they'll say they're originally from Montreal, Toronto, Kemptville, Arnprior, Renfrew or Pembroke. There's a reason Ottawa culture, in many ways, gravitated towards 'country living' because all those out-of-town bumpkins moved in and now the biggest attractions are rock bands from the eighties that pick-up-truck-driving husbands and cougar wives can dance and drink awkwardly to. A lot of red solo cups and air-punching going on at Ottawa concerts, and surely at TD Place.

But the Canadian Tire Centre started as the Palladium, then the Corel Centre, followed by Scotiabank Place and then its, for now, final destination; yet another corporate sponsor sucking the fun out of everything. It's not original to state how boring it is to have all the arenas with a business name pasted onto the banner but being unoriginal doesn't make it untrue. I always wished I could say 'Madison Square Garden' or the 'Boston Garden.'

Instead, Ottawa has an arena named after a home supplies megastore and it's parked way the hell out on the edge of town, unlike the best arenas which are always nestled right in the heart of downtown.

'Remember when we saw Drake there?' Macy said.

'Of course, that was fucking sick.'

'He was so good, oh my God.'

'Remember when Miguel opened for him?'

'He was amazing. And he's so hot, oh my God.'

'Yes, he is,' I laughed. 'Do you remember when we were all watching him, and we were all standing?'

Macy's eyes perked up and she started smiling. She knew where I was going with this.

'And we're all grooving and we're all in it, and then I noticed that you had gone to the washroom. And like, I was so in my own world that I finally noticed that most of the people in our section had sat down for a bit, and I was the only one standing.'

Macy burst out laughing.

'And I'm like, well I can't like sit down because it'll look awkward that I'm sitting because of them and I'll be embarrassed, but I can't keep standing because that's even more awkward, and everyone here'll think I'm gay and I'm obsessed with Miguel.'

Macy was dying. 'That is sooooo you! Of course, you kept standing!'

I smiled. 'Of course, I did. I did the weirdest shit and kept standing. I'm just grooving and not giving a shit and just in it, and then you come back and you're like why are you the only one standing?'

Macy was tearing up from laughing. 'And you finally sat down and I'm like everyone probably thinks you're gay.'

'I don't give a shit if they did. Miguel's a handsome dude.'

'And it's not the first time people thought you were gay.'

'That's true. I don't care. Didn't know you were homophobic.'

Macy scoffed. 'Yeah okay. I'm homophobic. You gonna cancel me now?'

'No, that's boring. I don't cancel people for innocuous remarks made in private. That's the stupidest shit ever.'

'Okay, you don't need to go on a rant about cancel culture.'

'I won't, believe me. It's no fun… Drake was amazing though.'

'Grandma was sick in the hospital when we went.'

I went silent for a beat.

'That's right, I forgot about that. Mom went three years before and your grandma went a few weeks after that, right?'

'Right… she forced me to go to Drake that night. She like insisted.'

'I remember. It was nice of her to do that. She knew you

needed a break. And you were so excited to see him.'

Macy started going through her Spotify to find a Drake song.

Canadian Tire Centre used to be a place for hockey games and concerts, ice shows and Disney spectacles; now, just a centre like any other for vaccinations. Driving by, it was weird to always see the parking lot barren. The place might as well have closed down.

Ottawa audiences were sitters, not standers. At shows, the only ones where everybody was standing for the whole time and were immersed in the music, and dancing and singing every rhyme were hip-hop and R & B shows. The rock and country shows had the requisite drinking (always light beer) and dancing (usually cowboy boot stomping and line dancing in miniature), but there was far more sitting going on. Ottawa was sleepy that way. It would be a common occurrence to go to an Ottawa concert and find couples sitting in their chairs; the guy with his legs crossed and the girl nuzzled up against him, his arm around her, their heads mildly bopping, with some barely audible 'whooo' sounds coming after each song. Not that there was anything wrong with mellow viewing, but a concert wasn't supposed to be like watching Netflix in your basement; it was supposed to be about losing your inhibitions and getting nasty; grimy.

You would find patrons saying inexplicable shit like, 'I paid for this seat so I'm going to sit in it.' What the fuck does that even mean? Canadian Tire Centre had a vibe that absolutely reeked. You had to fight to squeeze a robust atmosphere out of that place if you weren't at a hip-hop show. When a rapper was performing, you knew the place would be exploding and that everybody there was on point; any other occasion, you had to work to make it exciting in there. The place felt like a condemned luxury hotel.

All around the place were the usual arena checklist items. Corporate sponsors everywhere you looked; obscenely overpriced food and beverages; Hot 89.9 van outside trying to coax a 'good time' out of everyone going in; socio-economic hierarchy inside.

The inside had the usual formation of seating in which you were told loud and clear that if you had more money than others, you were worthy of better seating and better treatment. The thing that always baffled me is that people were generally okay with that line of thinking. Yes, if you have more money, you are worth more than others and have more value. As if box seats were not enough where investment bankers and CEOs could hob-nob and ignore the event, while they schmoozed and drank like fish, the arena invented 'Club Bell,' a noxious VIP and members-only section in which patrons could pay more and simulate the experience of being in their basement in a recliner chair. Essentially, you sit there eating a prime rib dinner and wine, being waited on the entire time, and you can have the choice of taking your shoes off and watching the game or concert, taking the occasional nap if the mood strikes. The feeling of being in a Shakespearean 'in the round' theatre, this was not. It was not sufficient to make people feel inadequate about being poorer than others, but the corporate mandate was to make them feel worthless as well, and less than happy during the experience since they had to spend their bi-weekly pay cheque on nosebleed seats. But the powers that be always threw the line out there that, 'there isn't a bad seat in the house.'

'What was the last thing we saw here?' Macy said, while she was still shuffling through Spotify.

'Paw Patrol Live with Daisy.'

Macy laughed. 'Oh my God, you're right. That was like two

years ago before the VID.' Her head was still down looking at her playlists.

'Before the VID. You got it. We can go there in a couple of weeks to get our first dose though.'

'That's right,' Macy beamed. 'If the anti-vaxxer protests don't get in the way.'

Sigh… I wasn't sure what it was for though.

CHAPTER SEVENTEEN

I had never spent any time in hospitals when I was a kid. Macy had practically lived inside hospitals, due to her grandfather, a Second World War veteran, interned in hospitals for much of his twilight years with a laundry list of mercurial cancers. Macy once told me that each Christmas until she was twelve, when her grandfather passed away, she would ask, 'Are we going to spend Christmas in the hospital this year?'

Having grown up in Blackburn Hamlet in the East End, the insular world of the suburbs reigned supreme. We were invincible and hospitals were something to see on television. I was twenty-seven years old, bordering on twenty-eight, when I fractured my right leg during an indoor soccer match on the usual Wednesday in which our rec league would play. We would play at revolving schools around the city, elementary and high, from Farley Mowat to St. Joseph's, and this particular game was at Bell High School around Bell's Corners.

I was rushed to Queensway-Carleton Hospital by a couple of my teammates. It was a hospital close by and it was indeed a *hospital*. I could smell sickness everywhere. In all directions, there was misery and fatigue. Nurses, both male and female, who looked like they hadn't showered or shaved in days, running from one operatory to another, simply doing their duty since they had no emotional engagement at this stage; at least that's how it looked. There were old old people and young young people, and a lot of helplessness in between. How many people could get afflicted with something and all seemingly simultaneously?

The waiting rooms were tin cans with the lids halfway off; sharp enough to still cut your thumb. People would ask the admins two questions usually: a) when are we going to get in? and b) what's the wi-fi password?

The smell though. A combination of hand sanitizer with stale bedspreads peppered with perspiration and topped with a likely psychological aroma of the putrid end. Hospitals were the only place in which a person could safely be in a space where the concept of 'the end' was very real and very likely. To be in a cemetery is different; the end has passed and you're into positive integers now, point zero having been life itself. The resting places are, as cliché would have it, peaceful and closed. Hospitals are full of pain, anguish, suffering, and anxiety about 'the end.' All the signs praising front-line workers during COVID were apt; they cannot be praised enough for enduring the catastrophe of 'the end' as a quotidian job requirement.

I sat in the waiting room with my leg up. Then got moved to an X-ray room. And then to another waiting room. And finally, the doctor showed up and told me my leg was broken. I thought I was invincible. How could this happen?

The cast went all the way up my leg up to my hip and would stay there for a month and a half, and then the cast would get cut in half so I could bend my leg, for another month, and judgement day would see the cast come off completely.

It was a flashy Spring day in May when I went to Queensway-Carleton Hospital to get the godforsaken cast taken off. They sawed it off with a contraption that they ensured would just cut through the fabric and not my actual leg; they were not lying.

When they ripped the cast off, I quietly gasped at the sight of my leg. It had shrunken down to a third of its width and looked like a dead animal, with sweat, grime, and matted hair abound. They gave me soap and a washcloth to clean the ghastly mess, and I proceeded to soap and scrub and itch my leg for the full allotted five minutes they gave me. When they said time was up, I asked for more. The sensation of itching and cleaning something so filthy took on a level of satisfaction that I don't think I had experienced before. The only thing preventing me from tearing up any more than I already had when I saw my stick figure leg, was the delirious mad scientist feeling of trying to itch my leg out of existence.

I put my Adidas on, grabbed the physiotherapy leaflet (I declined to come in for actual treatment and elected to do it myself at home; the idea of coming back to this woozy sanatorium was beyond bearable), and got out of Dodge.

The walk out of that hospital was one of the most glorious in my life. I called my parents who were in Germany and told them that my ordeal was over, for the most part. They asked if anyone was picking me up and I said no. I carefully boarded the OC Transpo articulated bus and sat down. The sun beamed down on my stubbly face. I got off early so I could walk around downtown. The leg was still iffy, but I did that thing that people never do any more; walked just to walk. I didn't have anywhere to be.

I never would have known it but around two years later, I would be back in that inferno. Not for myself, but to see my mom melt away from ovarian cancer, fighting an invisible invader. An entire life spent outside of hospitals but back to the Queensway-Carleton we went, and then off to the Ottawa General, which was close to where Macy grew up, and then finally to the Elizabeth Bruyere facility where they put you in a holding pattern until you can enter the void.

On Mom's second last day, Darius was in the Byward Market with his dad, very close to the facility, and they had scooted over to the Shafali restaurant to get some curried goat and biryani.

Darius said, 'What do we do? How long does Mom have?'

His dad answered, 'I don't know.'

Darius realised it was a stupid question and an inappropriate one to ask. If she was in the Elizabeth Bruyere, likely not very long.

They sat there on the semi-indoor, semi-outside nature of the Byward Market restaurants. Patios but not quite as it still looked and felt like they were sitting in a diner in which all the windows had been smashed to pieces.

They could see a lineup outside the Beaver Tails food truck one way and could hear a busker somewhere close by. The sound of sporadic cheering, clapping, and asking/demanding money from viewers. There was a delicate tinge of gasoline in the air, either from a leaky car driving by or perhaps from the busker show's fire-breathers.

Darius and his dad just sat there eating freely and easily; not once had they appreciated the ability to simply eat something without having to worry about vomiting it up again because your insides had caved in like a coal mine. Darius had felt that a couple of years before when his leg shattered but the inherent trait of taking things for granted had slowly crept back.

The Indian food was good but neither cared nor commented on it. Ten minutes down the road, there was a suffering angel trapped inside a room trying to eat something but unable to do so, with the full knowledge that the concept of the 'last meal' was over and done with. Her last meal had come and gone, and there would be no more meals. Not much more of anything else.

Darius and his dad walked slowly up the main drag not saying a word. Darius peered over at the Blue Cactus restaurant where just two years before he had hung out with Macy, when they had just been friends and co-workers at the time and drank strawberry daiquiris and prairie fire shots. Hers was tasty; his was disgusting but he wanted to look like a guy's guy, and not a girlie drinker. It was all quite silly in the end when she wanted a girlie guy all along and he wanted a tough manly girl.

Darius looked down Clarence Street and spied Wasabi where the family had gone to have sushi together when his brother had graduated from higher education. Fried ice cream. The ByWard Market was hopping and neither cared. Ottawa was beckoning us with some life and music and gasoline but all they wanted to do was go and sit by her bedside and sing her to sleep. Pump her full of dilaudid so she could whisper between the winds. At least so she wouldn't have to smell that hospital smell any more.

The sound of the buskers again. And people clapping. Darius wondered if those buskers had an actual job or if this was their full-time job? If it was, did they also get welfare cheques? How could they have a decent quality of life if they just busked for cash? It seemed like a different gig from sausage vendors, usually Polish guys, who would make a significant amount, it seemed. People always had appetites and needed lunch. People didn't necessarily need to see fire-breathing uni-cyclers who juggled melons. The bratwursts that sausage guy used to sell at the University of Ottawa campus on Laurier were spectacular. Darius, for one moment, felt joy. He forced it to dissipate.

CHAPTER EIGHTEEN

I loathe Kanata. It's one of those places where the bourgeoisie's worst instincts get honed and blasted, right into each other's faces. What was once bushland transformed, via digging and detonation, into Ottawa's version of a gated community for the upper-middle class. True gated communities do exist in Ottawa. Rockcliffe Park and Rothwell Heights are great examples of tucked-away 'utopias' in which the owners live in homes six times the usual size and amass exorbitant wealth simply to do their best William Randolph Hearst impersonations.

Explaining the futility and depravity (too strong a word?) of a gated community to one who lives there is a complete fool's errand. They will likely spout some Horatio Alger trash at you or pontificate on the evolutionary spirit and top it off with a slag on Karl Marx. It gets you nowhere. You would likely have more success speaking to a religious fundamentalist than you would talking to a member of the alleged upper crust of Ottawa, or any other city for that matter. The demonic countenance of one who relishes amassing wealth while others dumpster dive is one I cannot fully fathom.

Kanata is a low-rent version of those gated communities; filled with wannabe richies who wish they could afford that kind of life. Still loaded with those who live outside their means and take out two mortgages despite being well into six figures, closing in on seven.

Macy and I once were looking for an upgrade from our

condo in Riverside South to a home, preferably a town house. We reluctantly looked at a house in Kanata with these two 'hosts' who went on and on at length, bordering on temporal tumescence, about how massive the lawn is (why would I want to mow all that?) and how huge the shed is (I'm Brown; I don't know how to fix shit, and I have no supplies anyway) and how thick the granite countertop is (the thing was like a miniature boat in the middle of the kitchen; I was borderline afraid of the thing) and how space was an issue (this place was massive; what are you planning, a fucking hoedown?).

In Kanata, the concepts of 'getting ahead' and 'keeping up with the Joneses' are not just homespun folksisms; they are legitimate MOs that give these Kanata residents reasons to be. A Kanata citizen has no problem calling by-law officers on a neighbour who is using a clothesline in their backyard to hang wet clothes because it 'diminishes property value'. In essence, what they're saying is that it looks like something 'trashy' people would do so keep that shit out of our neighbourhood, we're already living pay cheque to pay cheque just trying to keep up with these two mortgages so please put your shit in a washing machine. In their minds, only Jamaicans and people from the assorted islands would hang their clothes so, again, keep that shit out of our neighbourhood. The nationality permitted into Kanata are Chinese people and only because they are considered honorary white people out there; the way they tend to their gardens with such brutal diligence is a lesson to all the aesthetically vain in Kanata. The Chinese in Kanata garden, do tai-chi in their laneways, and walk all day and all night; subsequently keeling over when they're past a hundred years old. Longevity is a thing with them apparently.

Kanata is a place where parents will gladly choose a jagged

mountain rock for the exterior of their pools as opposed to a curved softer plastic. Is the former more pleasing to look at? Of course. Is the latter perhaps safer for infants and toddlers running around on slick pavement who don't want to eat a mouthful of river stone? I would venture a yes. These considerations do not enter the minds of the Kanata citizen. They will take visual vanity over the safety of their children in a flash. House after house, street after street. Two-car and three-car garages. Add-ons. 'Seasonal rooms', whatever the hell those are. Giant beds of flowers. Massive pools. Brick on the front of the homes and vinyl on the sides. Garages that inexplicably reach out all the way to the road, creating a hallway to the front door, almost diminishing the actual entrance. And streets of strangely out-of-place New Orleans style roofing concepts amid the cookie cutter designs.

Daisy was stirring.

'How long have we been driving?' Macy asked.

'About an hour. Maybe an hour and a half.'

'Seriously?'

'Hey, I'm going by you. You said you wanted to drive around and let her nap. I'm positive she'll have trouble sleeping tonight.'

'Don't worry about it. She'll be fine.'

We passed the AMC Kanata Centrum Cinema. The typical multiplex monstrosity with nothing wholly original to mention. Apart from the arcade-themed dynamic of modern cinemas, the appearance of on-demand popcorn, full dining options (at Lansdowne only I believe; who would be shocked by Glebe-ites wanting a full dinner theatre experience?), the serving of beer and full recliner seating that simulates, like Club Bell at the CT Centre, the experience of sitting in your basement watching Netflix.

Corporations finally figured out, especially during COVID,

what people had wanted all along – to never be around other people and, when outside, to be under the illusion that there is nobody around them at all. I don't mind getting on board with that personally. I do like people that inspire me but there are very few of those out there. The other ninety-five per cent are people I can handle in small doses and then I just want to chill with my wife and daughter, who always and unfailingly make days feel luminous.

'You know it's been like over two years since we saw anything in that cinema,' I said to Macy.

'I know... it's crazy.'

'I can't even remember what it was. Do you?'

Macy did a Rodin's thinker pose and I wasn't sure if she was actually thinking back or humouring me.

'I can't remember either. Maybe some comic book movie? Or a musical? I can't remember.'

'A musical? What would that have been? There's not that many of those.'

'Yeah, probably a comic book movie.'

'But we don't watch those. Would we have seen one of those in the theatre?'

'For real, I cannot remember at all.'

There was something we had seen together here while my dad watched Daisy for the night. It was one of those strange experiences that was so off the wall, I didn't even care about the movie any more.

Macy and I walk into the cinema and it's like we're immediately thrust into Afghanistan. Lights are blaring and the sounds of bombs are going off everywhere around us. Kids are running around; some with no shoes on. Parents are chasing after them. People are standing at the self-checkout ticket line while others are waiting impatiently. Nobody wants to cause a delay at the machine for fear of looking like a Luddite; the biggest sin of the Millennial generation and one deserving of the guillotine treatment to Generation Z.

People mill about and see film magazines, for free, sitting on metal holders. Most people walk by these old relics with fascination. Paper held together with staples are not what most people want to use to pass the time when their smartphones with enough LED capability to illuminate the Champs Elysees are right in front of them.

The obligatory lineup to get popcorn, candy and gargantuan sodas queue up. And nachos with goopy diarrhoea cheese. Whose brilliant marketing idea was it to have nachos served at a movie theatre? Not that other patrons aren't already relentlessly irritating with their phones that they never turn off despite the ad prefacing the trailers beseeching all assholes and potential non-assholes to please turn your phones off. But to serve nachos? So, each monumental and ear-splitting crunch is enough to deafen each adjacent patron? And a faux cheese reek potent enough to render the faux butter stench on everyone's popcorn irrelevant.

Macy would say to me how I wasn't being fun when it came to movie theatres. I tried not being misanthropic but seeing a movie in a Kanata multiplex was like having all of your phobias packed into a sardine can and then pried open centimetre by centimetre. I wanted to enjoy that experience, but I guess everybody had different ideas of fun.

What Macy taught me was to enjoy even shitty experiences like these. Instead of stewing in toxicity, it was better not to be the enemy of fun. I had a friend once from France who was severely anti-religious, but he went to Midnight Mass once with his Catholic friends because he was invited. I asked him how it went, and he replied in classic Parisienne, 'It was funnnnn.' Not in a patronising way or an obnoxiously superior way. Just fun.

Macy showed me that straddling high and low fun, whatever those categories meant, was the way to truly have fun in this world and enjoy each day as opposed to just tolerating them.

I was waiting at the entrance of Cinema 16 for Macy for what felt like thirty minutes. She insisted on getting in line to get popcorn and water, so I said okay. I waited and waited. The curtains parted. Seven ads played with about eight hundred edits in five minutes. Still no Macy. The trailers came and went. No Macy. The movie itself started and I was borderline apoplectic. I was torn between watching the opening of this film and adhering to my duty of being pissed off at my wife for putting concessions ahead of the actual reason we came to the cinema.

Finally, after fifteen minutes of the film had played out, Macy saunters along with her popcorn and bottle of Dasani water.

'Where were you?'

'Getting this.'

It always amazed me when people didn't realise they were being disrespectful. Putting one's own desires (food and beverages) over another's (watching the fucking film from its beginning) was something I couldn't figure out.

'We've missed like fifteen minutes of the movie.'

'Oh. Okay let's go in.'

I was stoic as I attempted to keep it together.

'The theatre is pitch black. I can't see a goddamn thing.'

'Our seats are way up there. They're reserved.'

'We can't go up there now. There're people in those seats now and I can barely see it from here. We'd have to go up there and get in everybody's way and kick those guys out of their seats. I'm not doing that.'

'What's the big deal? We'll go up there.'

'Hell no. We'll just sit down there near the front where there's nobody.'

'That's too close.'

'Macy, you took forty-five minutes to get that smelly shit and now you want to make demands on where we sit? I'm not inconveniencing a bunch of people up top when we're now twenty minutes into the movie. We'll just sit down there.'

'Okay if you say so.'

She was so cheery. I couldn't understand it. We sat down and attempted to orient ourselves into the world of whatever bullshit we were watching. I purposefully declined to use the recliner option just out of spite thinking that people around me would wonder why I wasn't using it; like others would actually notice or give a shit.

I was trying to bring my anger level down and try to immerse myself into the film. There were iPhones bright everywhere with people who had paid to see this film and for some reason weren't even paying attention to it. There was the aroma of kernels, sugar, fromage and beer all around me, people chatting, texting, posting. It didn't seem like what the auteurs of the past had in mind when they spent years of their lives toiling away, surviving on bread and wine, to make a film to make the human experience incandescent.

And when I was still sitting at a mild boil, Macy turned to me and charmingly asked, 'Hey, how do you recline these things?'

I looked at her with a dead stare and continued watching the film. She shrugged her shoulders and munched away, enjoying every minute.

It was at that minute that I achieved a mini epiphany. This *was* fun. This communal experience of people hanging out together to watch something, each bringing a different point of view to it, was kind of refreshing. Why be hateful about it?

I couldn't refuse Macy anything for more than a minute, so I leaned over to her and whispered, 'It's that button down there and the one right under it.'

Macy, alerted to this, used the buttons and shifted into a recliner position; the final destination of all Kanata cinemagoers. She smiled right at me and offered me some popcorn, which I took with no obligation.

It was moments like these when I realised that being with Macy had made me into a better person. A more tolerant one; more merciful; more positive. More likely to label another as an enemy of fun rather than myself and what I used to be.

When the movie was over, popcorn buckets only housed yellow residue and coffee-coloured pellets, wrappers were under foot and phones burst into life with stored up potential energy; Macy and I smiled at each other.

A guy next to me tapped me on the shoulder and said, 'I don't know about that one. That was weeeeeird. Not my favourite, that's for sure. What'd you think?'

'I thought it was pretty cool. Definitely weird though. I kinda like that though.'

The guy smiled not feeling any defensiveness or a demeanour of having felt condescended to, as that wasn't my intention in the least. He didn't like it, but I did. That was really all there was to it.

'Have a good one,' he said to me, as he walked off in his steel-toed boots and Cabela's hat. I nodded and smiled at him.

'You ready, love?' I asked Macy.

'Let's wait for the herd to pile out,' she replied.

She exited the recliner position ready to go back out into minus forty-degree temps with wind chill.

CHAPTER NINETEEN

We were trekking home. Daisy's head had moved from the back of the car seat headrest to slightly forwards. She was releasing herself from her deepest version of slumber and was quietly tiptoeing into the world again. Not fully there yet but her mouth wasn't agape any more. Her eyes remained closed, but her lips were fidgeting about; burrowing for something it appeared.

'Hey love, I think she's waking up,' Macy alerted me.

'Yeah, I can see her.'

My eyes had become accustomed to darting back and forth from road to rear-view, road to rear-view, blind spot, road, rear-view, road. Make sure our baby is safe and make sure other drivers don't kill us.

'Look,' Macy nudged.

It was Daisy's daycare before she moved onto Steve MacLean Public School in our neighbourhood. My eyes slightly misted.

'Seriously?' Macy said to me, bordering on ridicule when she saw my eyes droop in liquid.

I forgot which author had said that the best relationships were the ones in which the female was masculine, and the male was feminine. That seemed like us. Macy could fix things around the house, and I liked to listen to Broadway musicals on Spotify. Not that gender roles were that concrete, but it sometimes felt reassuring to dwell on traditional modes. Even though it was clearly hateful, at least it wasn't complicated. Some days, I wouldn't even mind getting called a 'Paki' or a 'terrorist'. At least I knew who I was and who my attackers were. In a twisted sense, it gave me a pinch of serenity.

'What? I haven't seen it in a long time. We never go this way. I miss that daycare.'

'I know. Me too.'

Before Macy and I made the decision to have a child, we made a pact to say goodbye to our previous life and to say good riddance to it. It was a life of self-indulgence and flakiness. It was time to put somebody else entirely before us. To love someone more than we loved ourselves. Those who deem others 'helicopter parents' are ones who have not made this pact. Children are the cumbersome accessories in their quotidian existence. There are those parents who will not adhere to a change in their lives. They will stay who they were and will not deviate. If you are a parent and you do not feel a giant sea change in your personality and habits, you have failed.

To be a good parent, you must change. You must be someone entirely new. If you're the same, you are not committing enough to the game. When people speak of 'challenges', it goes without saying that they, nine times out of ten, are speaking of work challenges. They are never talking about the challenges of being a better spouse or a better parent. Those challenges are not even considered by most parents; they seem provincial to them.

If the true global pandemic is indeed bad parenting, then Macy and I were on a mission to change it in our house. By sending one good girl out into the world who might stand up for other kids who couldn't defend themselves; a girl who showed others respect and also had it for herself in abundance. Why are most kids assholes? The answer is simple: their parents are assholes. Assholes beget assholes. It's a modern story of Biblical proportions.

The Educara Daycare we put Daisy in was a Montessori. Macy and I were okay with spending twice the amount we would at a traditional daycare for this added care. It was the best money we ever spent. Instead of taking a trip down south, we felt that parents would be better served by putting their kids into a more caring and worthwhile daycare. It seemed more than palatable.

On one Halloween morning, the kids at the Montessori were dressing up. Daisy was to be Belle in her lovely lemon-coloured dress, with a crown and wand. Macy had left the costume on the bed and had neglected to mention it, but I had forgotten altogether that it was dress-up day at Daisy's daycare.

We drove there and I noticed that two other kids who had arrived were dressed up. My heart sank. I had forgotten Daisy's costume. I had two options; either leave Daisy there with no costume and get to work on time, or drive back home, get Daisy's costume, make sure she was ready to go, and then get to work late. For me, the decision was easy; it took me no time to figure it out.

I apologised to Daisy and told her to chill and wait for me while I dashed home to get the Belle dress and scoot back to get her ready. When I arrived and Daisy's eyes beamed, it was such a soul-stirring moment for me. I put the dress on her, and she marched into the daycare toddler room dressed up like all the other kids. She felt included and warm. I gave her a big kiss and a huge hug. I waved on the drive out of the parking lot and got to work late. I couldn't give two shits about being late to work. Work was work and I was dedicated and focused. But, in my current universe, work would always be minor; a silly distraction. The notion of getting work emails on my phone was a joke. I disabled that without haste. When I was away from work, I was devoted to my wife and daughter. The sea change had happened with me. Transformation is such a sticky concept and only really happens in gradations, but it smashed my very core and opened up a better person when I held Daisy in the delivery room.

'What are you thinking about, love?' Macy enquired.

'Wandering.'

'What about?'

'Mademoiselle back there.'

Macy smiled.

As we passed the daycare, I recalled Daisy and her crew spending the entire week of activities making strawberry lemonade, strawberry scones and strawberry butter, so she and her friends could serve it all to their 'grand-friends', who lived in the retirement home next door, on the roof patio of the building. Daisy was decked out in her strawberry dress and pony for the occasion. She had mixed all week and she poured on the day. It reminded me of the first day I dropped her off there and when picking her up, she greeted me at the door with a turgid piece of Romaine lettuce slathered with Caesar sauce in her grip.

'Remember when she was eating that Caesar salad on her first day?' I said.

'Yes! She's like finally food that tastes like something.'

'Yeah, tough for a kid to eat bulgur and quinoa.'

The stereotypes about Millennials were true on this score. Consumption of food was a serious thing. Everybody threw around the terms 'steroids' and 'antibiotics' when it came to the rearing of livestock, but a more thorough examination would lead you to, not believe, but know that most food out there was designed to slowly murder us. And who knew if bulgur and quinoa were the answer. Who was to say if Monsanto hadn't buried those with some fast-acting DDT for some kind of overwhelming growth response. We had a friend who had never fed their kid fast food. That seemed like a stretch. Imagine going to a birthday party and your kid can't eat the pizza unless it has a gluten-free crust with farm-to-table tomatoes, grilled tempeh and cashew cheese. It would sound like 'Theatre of the Absurd' if I hadn't seen it a half dozen times.

CHAPTER TWENTY

We were crossing Vimy Bridge and into Riverside South, our home for the past decade. It was a standard suburb. I grew up in the suburbs, but Macy grew up in Elmvale which had parts that felt like a suburb but was generally fairly coarse.

Neither Macy nor I were suburb people. The neighbourhoods were overly quiet and sedate. The people were either extraneously jovial or completely dead inside; there was no magical middle. We were a bit of an anomaly as we had no problem socialising with anyone and everyone, but we generally avoided it if we could. If hell really was other people, then we were better suited to relaxing at home and enjoying each other's company.

We always found that those who ventured outside constantly had one or both of the following: a) a serious case of FOMO, and/or b) a genuine hatred of their own families.

There are those who think that things are actually happening out there and that there are amazing conversations they're missing out on; that really is not the case. There's nothing out there but hours and hours of domestic beer-laden bluster masquerading as conversation. A lot of blaming Trudeau for every ill in the country while making a definitive point about 'doing their own research' with respect to the new vaccines.

Macy and I, when on a patio with Daisy, would sometimes spy on the conversations at adjacent tables. What were they talking about when they weren't completely ignoring each other with their heads down into their phones? There was no special novelty in pointing out how strange it was to see people sitting across from each other, not talking to each other, and molesting their phones. Even a toddler would be able to notice that. And yet this strange behaviour still happens. How?

At restaurants, at the park, at the mall, in the neighbourhood... all people ever talked about was their work and their homes. The first part was about how much they either hated their jobs or how underpaid they were, or both. The second part was about how much their home was worth, how much it would be worth in a few years, what upgrades they had done and how they never had enough space. And then a third optional topic was how much they hated Trudeau.

Was hell really other people? It appeared that way to Macy and me. We saw a music star on YouTube doing this answer seventy or so questions and one thing she said was that COVID only made her realise that she's a homebody who is happier at home than out there. The bulk of society will look at a 'homebody' and will feel no shame in shaming them and labelling them as 'hermits'. Somehow, loving your family and wanting to be with them more than outsiders has taken on the mark of the scarlet 'A'.

'Shall I wake her up, Darius?'

'Yeah, she's getting up anyway.'

'How long's it been?'

'About an hour or so. Maybe a bit more.'

'That's not bad.'

'Naw, should be fine. We'll get settled, we'll read together, have some dinner, listen to Hot 89.9, play a bit, maybe do some karaoke and then get her ready for bed.'

'You always make fun of my karaoke and you guys don't even pay attention.'

'We do. It's just that you seem like you're boring yourself to sleep when you're doing it.'

'Fuck you.'

'Whoa. Okay, chill. When we're singing, we're just being casual about it. Do a song, dance a bit, you can mill about, groove a bit. We're not gonna like sit there and stare at the singer for the whole song. Especially when you're always singing ballads.'

'I like ballads and I'm better at them.'

'That's fine. But Daisy's looking for party songs, not torch songs.'

'What's a torch song?'

'Like a love song. I think that's what it means. I'm pretty sure. Like a soft kinda chill song.'

'What's wrong with that? Why do you and Daisy always have to make fun of me?'

'We don't. What are you on about?'

'It just feels like you both have like a little clique, and you make fun of me.'

'Macy, nobody makes fun of anybody in our house. That's what assholes do. If you wanna sing ballads, go for it. Sing what you feel like singing. It's just that Daisy wants to get amped, and those songs kinda bore her a bit. So, she starts getting restless. It's not a knock on you.'

'She should learn to respect what I'm singing though.'

'Macy, she does. But she is six. She's gonna start stirring if you don't sing something that'll engage her.'

Macy was silent for a beat.

'Maybe I won't sing anything then.'

'God, you're going fight or flight now? Sheesh.'

I made sure to do the 'sheesh' with a high-pitched upturn like one of the hip-hop songs Macy liked. It, like always, did the trick. She smiled and I was happy. Little stimulus and response emotional catharsis was all we ever needed.

CHAPTER TWENTY-ONE

On our left, houses that didn't used to be there. The right, flat grassland that is now a pile of soil, bricks and yellow construction company vehicles. Where there is space, condos shall rise. If futurists are correct and, in five hundred years, population growth will have become so exponential and pronounced that we will all be standing shoulder to shoulder... Well, I don't have a fascinating conclusion to that. Except that that thought is fucking terrifying. Well, not for us so who gives a shit, right?

Strange to see a neighbourhood, a suburb, that is so devoid of any character and be resigned to the fact that this is where we'll be for the next two decades of our life. Macy always wants to move to Montreal or Rome or London. It's not just that she is romanticising the notion or that it's completely impractical... it is just those things. You must be a special kind of person to uproot your existence like that. Not necessarily special; just different. Those people who can go to a new city as a tourist and, in their natural crusading style, stumble upon adventure after adventure, can truly catch the fun in a trip. But then there are those pitiful buffoons who think they have that same ability so they dump themselves into a metropolis to have 'adventures' but it's so against their nature that they essentially amble around the city bored out of their minds, attempting to find a 'hole in the wall' restaurant that they can boast to their friends and family about, before begging to go back to the hotel.

Macy and I are somewhere in the middle. We have that

spontaneous spark to explore but at the same time, we know our risk limitations and are perfectly content to plan a trip meticulously and then hope to hang organically found adventures off of this framework. It has always worked, happy to report.

Riverside South is a suburb like all others. There are a couple of mini-malls, houses are going up and condos are being renovated and rented. There's a Catholic high school, a couple other elementary schools, some fields, splash pads, play structures, manicured lawns, dopes walking their pets at all hours who think you don't notice when they don't pick up their pets' shit heaps. Circle K convenience stores and pharmacies. Crossing guards and 40 km/hr signs on side streets to limit speeding assholes' proclivity for potentially killing small kids. Luckily though, there's a bridge to Barrhaven which extends to the highway and there's Limebank Road which busts off into Riverside Drive, which can take you places that are actually interesting. Riverside South is a place to flop; best thing is it's five minutes' drive to get out of there.

Our town house was approaching. Daisy's eyes were ever so slowly prying themselves open.

Macy suddenly blurted out, 'Riverside South is our home.'

I retorted. 'It sure is.'

'The night Daisy was born, we walked around the condo on Beryl Private and tried to get the contractions going, up and down the hallways and stairs, around the condo blocks outside.'

'I remember.'

'And I sat on the toilet and some weird shit was coming out of me. The mucus plug I think.'

'Yeah, that was really delightful. I liked how I was forced to see it.'

'And we hopped on out and a day or two later, we hopped

back and carried the car seat up the stairs.'

'That thing was fucking heavy too. Like a goddamn anvil.'

'And we started losing sleep.'

'But then we got it back again.'

'And then Daisy was cluster-feeding, so my tits were getting milked like vacuums.'

'And we started losing sleep again.'

'We fed her breast milk and formula.'

'Yeah, I think we got the paediatrician's memo wrong on that one. It was supposed to be mutually exclusive. Not a fucking dairy buffet.'

'And Daisy bulked up and her doc said she might be obese.'

'That bitch. The doctor, not Daisy.'

'But I loved her all roly-poly like that.'

'Me too. With her weight and her head-wrap, she looked like a Bulgarian serf… were there Bulgarian serfs?'

'She was rolling.'

'Not crawling. Too much weight.'

'Then she was walking.'

'Then she was running.'

'And when we'd go to play structures, we wondered why the other parents weren't playing with their kids.'

'I know. I never understood why every parent looked so mad and were either talking shit with other parents or on their phones. Your kids are trying to get your attention, assholes!'

'Then we'd get called "helicopter parents".'

'Fuck them. Who cares what they think?'

'I wish they'd be better at it.'

'God, me too. Preaching to the choir.'

'And you'd hold Daisy in your arms and walk around and around the kitchen island trying to get her to fall asleep.'

'Worked too. After about an hour.'

'And when she'd get her fever episodes and she'd get up in the middle of the night and puke, we'd be tag-teaming getting it cleaned up, getting Daisy to feel better, and cleaning the sheets and her pyjamas.'

'And I'd wear a T-shirt over my face and wrap it like I was in Kandahar.'

'Yeah, the smell.'

'Puke was the worst smell ever.'

'I think shit was worse.'

'Yeah, you thought shit was worse. That's why I was always on diaper duty, and you'd clean up the puke.'

'And then the medication started working and the fevers went away.'

'Thank God they did. And Allah and Buddha. And the Indian guy with blue skin and lots of arms.'

'And we moved out of the condo where she came to stay for the first time.'

'To the town house we went. Well, down the street really.'

'And she had more space to roam.'

'Yes, the space thing. People in the suburbs will not stand for no space. They won't tolerate cramped quarters. Bunch of Costco Malcolm X mother fuckers out here.'

'And her hair grew.'

'Until you cut it into a bob and made her look like a boy.'

'And we started renting the condo.'

'I know. We turned into little mini entrepreneurs.'

'And we played with Daisy. And read to her and wrote with her and painted with her.'

'And then she learnt to read and write and paint.'

'Do you want another baby?'

'I'm good, love. It's too perfect as it is. I don't want anything to fuck this dynamic up.'

'Me too.'

'Most families should have one child but most of them should have none at all because narcissistic mental defectives should not have children.'

'Remember at the condo when that Brown guy knocked on the door when he thought domestic violence was going on?'

'Oh my God, that fucking idiot! I finish work that day and it's pre-Daisy days. I'm watching the Wimbledon semi-final and I'm throwing my fist in the air and gettin' crazy and screaming, and I get a knock on the door. I was gonna ignore it like usual, but I look through the peephole and the Brown guy from downstairs looks really concerned and he's got his hand on one knee. I open it and he's like, "Is everything okay?" And I'm like, "Yeah." And he goes, "Is someone getting beaten in there?" I'm like, "No, I'm watching tennis and I'm cheering. There's nobody in here." And in my head, I'm thinking, who the fuck can't tell the difference between cheering sports and beating the shit out of somebody? I would've been offended if I wasn't totally fucking perplexed.'

'Then what happened?'

'I said, "Okay, bye." I'm like, "We're done here, right?" Then the next year when Malcolm Butler intercepted that ball on the goal line in the Superbowl and you're asleep on the couch and I'm running around the kitchen island screaming and shouting and cheering this miracle that just happened. Somewhere in my head, I'm like oh fuck. Is that Brown dude gonna come up here and interrogate me again? That's when I learnt to cheer softly and punch the air. And then when Daisy was born, all crazy cheering had to be quiet cheering so she wouldn't wake up. When you were asleep on the couch when Tom Brady led them back from 28-3, I did so much silent cheering, I had dogs lined up outside our front door.'

'You Brown guys.'

'Yes, us Brown guys.'

'You're all so loud and illogical.'

'You're one hundred per cent right.'

'Everybody in your family is crazy with the hand-talking and criticizing everything and thinking everybody's an idiot.'

'That's what being Brown is all about. They think everybody is a moron and they're going to sip cardamom tea, eat mixed nuts and dates, with a gigantic bowl of fruit in front of them that nobody is going to touch and will talk for five hours about how everyone on the planet is an ignoramus except for them.'

'It's tiring.'

'Dude, I grew up with that. You only married into it.'

'It's still tiring.'

'I had to beat that shit out of myself. That was the tiring part.'

'Riverside South blows.'

'No shit. But this is home.'

'Can we move to Rome?'

'Learn Italian.'

'Fuck that.'

'Okay then.'

'How about London?'

'No thanks. Too expensive and I'll always feel like an outsider there. I'll always be a Paki to them.'

'You're not even from Pakistan.'

'Then why have I been called one in my life? And they look at all Brown people the same anyway. Brown people are to the UK as Black people are to the US.'

'What does that mean?'

'The trash that the ruling majority in those nations hate. But it's not as overt as it used to be because Americans like hip-hop and Brits like curry.'

'Exactly, it can't be that bad if curry is huge there.'

'Just cuz they like curry doesn't mean they like the people who created it. They still want all the Brown people exterminated. The Brits can learn to make curry themselves. It's not that hard.'

'London would be good, I think.'

'Macy, they still have fucking royals. A goddamn queen. Can you imagine? A society that advocates for a fucking royal family. It's insanity. This is 2021. And the people there are okay with it. That's the shocking part. They're actually proud of having a backwards hierarchy right in their backyard.'

'My grandma liked the royals.'

'Yeah, those traditional values don't just go away. You think I'd ever feel at home in a country where the people take pride in the royals and the word 'Paki' gets tossed around like it's nothing? My uncle had to deal with local vandals trashing his pizza shop all the time. The UK is the source of so much of twentieth-century misery, it's crazy.'

'Okay, holy shit. This wasn't an excuse for you to start going on and on about this.'

'Sorry. Let's just say London is out.'

'How about Paris?'

'Learn French.'

'I know core French.'

'You mean you can conjugate to be and to have. That's not French. That's trash.'

'Kanata?'

'Kanata is Karen-land so no thank you.'
'God, no. I was kidding. I hate that place. Vanier?'
'If I wanna get shot.'
'Bayshore?'
'If I wanna get shot.'
'The Glebe?'
'We'd have to buy a dog.'
'Rockcliffe Park?'
'We'd have to buy a Bentley.'
'Rothwell Heights?'
'We'd have to buy a used Bentley.'
'Iris area?'
'We'd have to live in Ottawa Housing projects or old veteran homes that are like tin boxes.'
'Sandy Hill?'
'If I want my car upturned by frat boys.'
'That's only when the Ravens play the GeeGees.'
'Yeah, that's not good enough for me when you're saying it's still a possibility… and I don't want beer puke on my front steps.'
'Orleans?'
'Too far. And learn French.'
'Downtown.'
'Like where?'
'Where the government buildings are.'
'Closest apartments are near Bronson. And again, I don't wanna get shot.'
'Westboro?'
'Too many restaurants that are farm-to-table.'

Macy sighed. She finally said, 'How about Riverside South?'

'It's fucking wack but at least it's got good schools and Daisy can play anywhere she wants without finding used needles on the ground.'

'Yeah.'

'Yeah, that is a big deal. And she can play in a splash pad without finding a used condom in the drain.'

'Yeah.'

'And it's only a ten-minute drive to escape and the three of us go downtown to get a donair from Wolf Down.'

Macy smiled. 'Yeah, that is true.'

'If I knew the way to end this conversation was to just mention a donair…'

Macy's smile turned into a broad toothy grin. I spied the rear-view as we curb-bumped into the driveway. The car stopped; I put it in park. Push to start in reverse. My legs were sore from sitting. Daisy's eyes were open. I think they had been open for a few minutes, but she had been staring out the window. Both Macy and I turned around and Daisy turned to meet us with a quizzical expression on her face.

Daisy sputtered to life. 'Was I asleep?'

I said, 'Yes, my love, you were. You needed a nap, so we let you nap, love.'

Macy said, 'How do you feel?'

Daisy answered, 'Kind of hungry.'

I said, 'I'm too exhausted to cook anything tonight.'

'My goodness, me too,' Macy concurred.

Daisy said, 'Take-out?'

We all nodded.

She said, 'Subway?'

We nodded in the affirmative.

'Can we get it from the Indian guys around the corner?'

'Sure, love, we can order it from there.'

Macy said, 'Can we just do Skip the Dishes?'

'Yeah, sounds good. I don't want to drive any more.'

Daisy said, 'Can we listen to Hot 89.9 at dinner?'

We said sure.

Daisy asked, 'If we do Skip the Dishes, will it still be from the Indian guys around the corner?'

'Yes, love.'

She was as pleased as passionfruit punch.

I was glad we were home. I was glad we were healthy. I was glad we were hungry. I was glad we had electricity and heat. I was glad we would have food on the table. I was glad we had wi-fi.

Glad and relieved and happy.

CHAPTER TWENTY-TWO

Daisy was lying in bed. Nine p.m. as usual. Macy always said we put Daisy to bed much later than other parents. We were always baffled when parents said their kids went to bed at seven or seven thirty p.m. We thought other parents had no interest in actually spending time with their kids so they were over-eager to get them to bed so they could go and binge-watch something or work out. We chalked our bedtime routine up to a 'European' style. We were happy with that. We loved being with Daisy as much as possible so perhaps it was selfish of us to put her to bed so late. But was nine really late? When I was a kid, Iranian households on Saturday nights when the families would get together would go until two a.m. and we'd be in bed at three a.m. That was at about seven years old.

'Daddy.'
'Yes, love.'
'I'm not sure which stuffy to sleep with.'
'How about Big Snoof?'
'He was last night.'
'Whitey?'
'He was three nights ago.'
'You remember that far back?'
'Yes.'
'All right. How about Pastelly?'
'Okay. Pastelly.'

I handed her the diluted teal, yellow and pink fur-coated

stuffy, she tucked it under her arm, and her eyes slowly drooped and shut down.

'Good night, love. Have only sweet dreams and see you soon. If you have a bad dream, come and join us in our bed, yeah?'

'Okay, Daddy.'

I made the thumb gesture of the BTS Army heart sign, and she did it back. I lay down next to her on the ground until she was fully asleep. My eyes opened and closed, drifted in and out. I thought of nothing and, through no fault of my own, thoughts from work tried to creep in and I quickly batted them away with a fly swatter. All thoughts of that venal place were in the rear-view once I stepped into my car and drove home. Or in the COVID-era, logged off with my workstation on top of our dresser, while still in my pyjamas.

Thoughts of films and songs and smiles would pop into my head. My eyes were closed but I didn't realise in my faux reverie that Daisy was still awake.

Is Daddy asleep?

How many times does he wake up in the middle of the night to pee?

How come I don't have to?

How come I never pee in my pants?

If Daddy didn't get up to pee, would he pee in his pants?

Mommy and Daddy go to sleep after me and they get up before me. Do they not need a lot of sleep, or do I just sleep too much?

Cats sleep over ten hours a day, I think. Do they just dream all day?

What's that banging sound? Is it raindrops falling outside or is it Maurice from next door playing video games?

Daddy doesn't play video games, but he said that some grown-ups do sometimes. But Daddy said he played them when he was a kid. Why do grown-ups play video games? Aren't they supposed to be for kids?

Grandpa's stews are always really spicy. Why does he use so much pepper?

How many days until Christmas? I'll count the days tomorrow on my calendar. But how will I remember? If I get out of bed to write it down, will Daddy wake up? I don't want to step on him by accident. If I wake him up, he won't get mad though. He never gets mad. Some kids at school always say their parents yell at them and get angry. How come Mommy and Daddy never do? I think sometimes I don't listen, but they never get mad. I'm glad they never do. That would be horrible.

The lady at the place we get macarons has a gap between her teeth. If she wanted to get it fixed, she could go to a dentist. If she doesn't want to, maybe it doesn't matter to her. It might cost a lot of money though. Does she have a piggy bank? I could give her some of the coins from my owl piggy bank. There are like hundreds of coins in there. I don't need all of them.

I like jumping on the trampoline with my cousins. Boys play rough sometimes, but it was really fun anyway. I just didn't like when my nose bounced off the trampoline. It hurt for a second and I cried but not for very long.

If we had a cat, would it scratch me? I like them but what if it scratched up my stuffies and wrecked them? And get hair all over the place? Daddy is always vacuuming, and he'd probably go nuts if he saw all that cat hair in the house. I don't like the idea of them pooping and peeing in the house though. Maybe I could teach the cat how to use the toilet. I saw a YouTube video of a guy teaching his cat to do that.

It smells like onions in here. I think Daddy is farting in his sleep. He always gets onions on his subs. He said they're really good for you and people from Iran and places like that love onions. Daddy said they give things really good taste and they're really important. Bad thing is the farts all smell oniony and the door is closed. Should I go and open it a bit? Don't wanna wake Daddy up though. He's sitting in a fart cloud. It would be good for him too. Maybe just forget it. Can you choke on fart smells? Is it bad for your health? I'm not sure. I'll ask tomorrow. If I remember.

When is this tooth gonna fall out? Should I keep wiggling it? Will there be a lot of blood? Will the bloody tooth go under my pillow for the tooth fairy? What if blood gets on my bed? Will Mommy and Daddy clean the tooth first? Probably. But it's kind of weird having a body part in bed with me. Really weird. Guess it's okay since I'll get something. Like a dollar? Or maybe a stuffy? I think the tooth goes in a bag. A tooth bag. Mommy and Daddy got in online.

I need to remember to write a Christmas list for Santa. A stuffy, a book, an LOL and maybe a Hatchimal. And maybe a Magic Mixie.

If we went to the Amazon rainforest, there are so many animals that could kill you. Anacondas, red-bellied piranhas and poisonous dart frogs. Jaguars too. Those aren't creepy at least. Maybe one day we'll go there. I'm not sure though. Too creepy. It's not fun going somewhere filled with things that can kill you. I don't understand people who have fun being around things that can kill you. Why is it fun for them?

Are ancient mummies real? They're people who went to Heaven, but their bodies are still here and they're dead. They can't move anywhere. They're sleeping forever. But, when they're wrapped up like in Egypt, can they come back to life? It's a bit creepy to think about. Maybe I don't think about it any more.

Daddy shaves his head. If he didn't shave it, he would still have hair on the sides of his head but nothing on top. Daddy always says it would look a bit silly, so he shaves it all. He says he loves it and doesn't miss hair at all. Mommy has tonnes of hair. She looks like a lion. Because of COVID, she couldn't go and get a haircut, so she didn't have one in two years. Daddy always says he has to vacuum so much of her hair from the carpets. It's like she sheds like a wild cat.

Who should I invite to my birthday party? Will we do it at Mooney's Bay again? It was so fun. I don't want too many kids there. Just my best friends. Do I give them the invitations or do Mommy and Daddy text their parents? What if the kids said no? They would come though, I think. Birthday parties are fun. I wonder what the presents would be. Would COVID stop some kids from coming? All the kids are in school though so it should be okay. What if they said no? Would I care? I think I would.

Is one hundred plus one hundred two hundred or one thousand? I'll ask Mommy and Daddy tomorrow. I might have to write it down though, so I don't forget.

I wish I could eat McDonald's every night. Why do Mommy and Daddy say we can only have that every once in a while? Does it have bad things inside it? I don't think there's anything weird in it. It's just unhealthy. Like it could give you a heart attack and you would fall and maybe go to Heaven. Or it could really make you fart a lot. That's kind of funny. Not the heart attack but the fart part. McDonald's farts always smell like onions. Well, Daddy's anyway. Mommy and I don't eat onions. They taste too spicy on the hamburger.

I wonder if the Indian guys at the Subway have seen the Taj

Mahal. Has every Indian person seen it? It looks so cool. I would love to see it. And the Pyramids in Egypt. And the Great Wall of China. And Mount Fuji. Is it Fuji or Fiji? I can't remember. I should write that down, so I remember to ask Mommy and Daddy.

My cousin asked Daddy if it's better to work at a job you like for less money or to work at a job you don't like for more money. Daddy right away said that you should work for the job that you're happy at for less money. He said that money is important, so you don't struggle. Having money means you can have hot showers and cook your food at home without the company coming and turning your heat off. But he said money isn't so important that you should be miserable your whole life. I don't even want to work anywhere. Could I just go to school and live with Mommy and Daddy forever? I thought about maybe working at a zoo or working with a laptop like Daddy. Some kids in class said they want to be marine biologists. I'm not sure what that is but so many kids say it. Do they just say it to say it? I think it just means working with ocean animals and learning how they work. Like a veterinarian for ocean animals? But maybe I can live with Mommy and Daddy in our house forever. I don't want to move. Would they be okay with that? I'll ask them tomorrow if I remember. I should write it down.

CHAPTER TWENTY-THREE

Daisy had drifted into the pleasure void until the next morning. At about five thirty a.m., she would likely march into our room quietly and close the door loudly, before nestling between Macy and me, and due to our queen-sized bed, I'd be the one who would do the gentlemanly thing and retreat to the bottom of the bed and sleep in a ball, while my two queens lay resting with proper pillows and ample space.

Everything was quiet. The stillness of a home when your child has gone to bed is a disturbing thing. I could hear the walls creaking and the foundation of the home settling. The condensation building up between the panes of our old windows that probably needed replacing. How much would that cost? Probably a lot.

I walked to the kitchen and filled my water bottle. I sipped and then gulped the entire thing. Macy was waiting downstairs with tea. I would definitely be peeing in the middle of the night. Why did I drink so much? I read somewhere it was good to do that. But what about getting up and disrupting your sleep at three a.m.?

I closed the curtains and turned all the lights off, leaving the kitchen hood fan light on. I checked the front door, put the chain on and made sure the stove knobs were off; I did that task several times. I made sure the fridge and freezer were closed; the rubber squishing back and forth with each push. I used my hand to wipe all the crumbs off the counter and dumped them in the sink and rinsed them down. The food traps had something in them, and they stunk; I'd figure it out the next morning.

I walked downstairs into the basement. Clothes were hanging on the racks and my Patriots jersey was hanging off the mantel. Macy handed me a cup of cardamom tea and some smores-flavoured fudge we got from somewhere. I thanked her and sipped and chewed, sipped and chewed.

Macy rubbed my leg while I put on Netflix. There wasn't really anything I felt like watching. I just wanted to sit and sip and chew and breathe a lot; some heavy and some light. Macy was drinking her tea more forcefully and was watching TikTok videos on her phone.

She would swipe through them quickly and I wasn't even sure she was watching any of them when I'd glance over. How did she know so fast if it would be something she'd be interested in or not?

She leaned over and showed me one. I leaned over and watched it and laughed the laugh of someone very tired but very happy. Very content and very relieved and very put together.

It was funny. For every nineteen TikTok videos that were awful and uninspired, there would be one, like the one Macy just showed me, that would be a gem; that made watching all of the other trash ones worth it.

Macy put her head on my lap with her tea resting on her belly and her phone up in the air. When she bellowed with laughter, I could feel the rumble of her vocal cords on my scrotum. It was kind of arousing.

I breathed deeply and then went back to a normal cadence. The salad days were vapour, but I was here and very much alive. Alive and present. Present and glad. It was the most glorious and perfect nervous breakdown one could ever imagine.